# The Run for the Elbertas

# The Run
# for the Elbertas

## JAMES STILL

Foreword by Cleanth Brooks

THE UNIVERSITY PRESS OF KENTUCKY

Some of the stories in this volume first appeared in *The Atlantic Monthly*, *Mountain Life and Work*, *North Georgia Review*, *The Saturday Evening Post*, *The Yale Review*, *The Virginia Quarterly Review*.

ISBN: 0-8131-1414-4 (cloth); -0151-4 (paper)

Library of Congress Catalog card no. LC 80-51019

Scholarly publisher for the Commonwealth,
serving Berea College, Centre College of Kentucky,
Eastern Kentucky University, The Filson Club,
Georgetown College, Kentucky Historical Society,
Kentucky State University, Morehead State University,
Murray State University, Northern Kentucky University,
Transylvania University, University of Kentucky,
University of Louisville, and Western Kentucky University.

*Editorial and Sales Offices:* Lexington, Kentucky 40506

*For*
*Iris Grannis and Guy Loomis*

# Contents

# Foreword

This collection of James Still's stories—*The Run for the Elbertas*—is doubly welcome. It makes generally available in book form pieces of highly interesting Americana and it also goes far toward insuring that an excellent contribution to our literature will not be lost to sight. When *On Troublesome Creek,* from which several of these stories are taken, appeared in 1941 it received the acclaim of the thoughtful and sensitive reader. So had Still's novel, *River of Earth,* published a year earlier. But Still's literary virtues are solid and quiet, not flashy and sensational. Still's work needs to be absorbed by the reader and by a considerable body of such readers before it can take its due place in the accepted canon of our literature.

Many of the tales in the present volume are told by a boy who is eight or nine years old in the early stories, ten or eleven in later ones. His stories—and the others—all have to do with happenings in the Kentucky mountains, presumably in the 1920s.

Most readers will be startled by the revelation of such primitive life still surviving in the southern Appalachians at so late a time. Yet if present-day Americans are to understand themselves, they need occasionally to step out of what we like to think of as the rushing mainstream of American life. Life in a backwater community may provide an illuminating glimpse into the older America, the frontier America, which was a necessary preliminary stage of our present civilization.

The culture depicted in Still's book, though quite primitive, is not brutish; in such a culture men have to be ever mindful of the elemental facts on which their very existence depends but they do not allow those pressures to make them inhuman. In fact, the people who live along Still's mountain creeks are actually more warmly human than many of the men and women who live the more insulated life of our great cities. For they are to each other never mere cyphers—they are always fellow creatures, if sometimes all too human—even on occasion downright ornery.

The boy who narrates several of the stories is the perfect observer through whose eyes we are allowed to see this old-fashioned world. He has a boy's curiosity and freshness of vision. He is alert and properly inquisitive about the world in which he finds himself. He is an "innocent" in the pristine sense of that word, yet nevertheless a realist. The terms here are not contradictory: the boy has no illusions that the world is less than harsh or that life is easy. The people of the stories are never far away from real hunger. They live far below what we now know as the poverty line, but that circumstance has not destroyed their basic good humor or sense of hope. All of them seem to find life good and living a joy.

What one notices at once is the language used in these stories. It is idiomatic, highly concrete, richly metaphoric, and has the true lilt of oral speech. It is not precisely the dialect that Faulkner's novels have made familiar to so many twentieth-century readers, for it has its own peculiar characteristics. Yet there is a large overlap with Faulkner's and with the "Southern" dialect in general.

"Nary" for "never a," for example, is common among the country people throughout the South. So is "hit" for "it"—a survival of the Anglo-Saxon form—among the folk, black and white. So also is the occasional survival of obsolete forms like "boughten" for "bought." (Robert Frost's old-fashioned New Englanders also use it: see his brilliant little poem "Provide, provide.") Another feature of this dialect is its preference for compound terms like "gamble cards," "lie-tale," and "sun-ball," "moon-ball," and "earth-ball."

Yet Still is sensible in not requiring that his readers struggle through a thicket of dialect spellings, with elisions and dropped letters marked by inverted commas. For instance, he does not even indicate the dropped *g*'s in such words as "going," "doing," and "living," though one may be sure that the dropped form is general among his speakers. As their rimes show, even Wordsworth, Coleridge, Byron, Shelley, and Keats dropped their *g*'s. In fact, the dropping was general in English until the Victorian schoolmarm restored the *g* sound under the influence of the spelling.

To give the flavor of the dialect, Still is content to rely on the use of occasional dialect words such as "mort" or "bunty" or "roust," plus folk expressions such as "I'm a hicker-nut hard to crack," or "couldn't make a hum-bird a living," or "it would take Adam's grands and greats to rid that ground." One must not assume, however, that these Southern highlanders have either debased the English language or coined a new language all their own.

Many of their peculiar words go back to older forms of the standard language or to the British county dialects. Consider the three words I have instanced above. "Mort," meaning a great deal of something, is characterized by the *OED* as "dialectal"; Dickens has one of his characters use it in *David Copperfield*. "Bunty" seems to be derived from "bunting," meaning "swelling or plump." The Scottish antiquary Robert Jamieson cited its use by the folk of Roxburghshire who called a plump child a "buntin brat." "Roust" in the sense of "rout out" is again characterized by the *OED* as "dial. and U.S." So it goes.

The ordinary reader, of course, will hardly be disposed to look up such words in the *OED* or in the special dialect dictionaries, nor need he do so in order to enjoy these stories. The context will usually indicate the basic meaning. Furthermore, the derivation of many of these expressions is transparent. Thus "whiter than a hen and biddy dish" obviously refers to a white china dish, the cover of which is shaped like a hen brooding her chicks, the "biddies," one or two of which are usually represented peeping out from under her feathered body. When Peep Eye asks "Air you been dranking john corn?" she is referring to whiskey, which in Burns's Scotland was called "John Barley Corn." But barley was not the grain used in the Kentucky mountains. It was plain corn (maize); hence "barley" properly dropped out.

Why do I put such emphasis on Still's language? Because it is central to what his stories so powerfully render: the ways of a culture which sharply differs from that of twentieth-century urban America. Any culture is most deeply and sensitively reflected in its language. There we find the expression of its central concepts and its basic modes of feeling. If we are to be given an insider's view of that culture—that is, if we are to be made to experience it as the person within it does, we must enter it through his language.

I remember having witnessed in Chicago thirty-odd years ago a play about mountain folk of North Carolina. It may have been originally written from an insider's point of view, but once it was deemed to have possibilities for a Broadway production, the play doctors got to it and "improved" it for the benefit of the urban outsider. The play now stressed the quaintness, bawdy realism, and provincial depravity of its characters. The aim became titillation at the bizarre speech and sexual activities of a culture to be viewed as comically decadent.

There is no nonsense of this sort in *The Run for the Elbertas*. The people in these stories take their culture for granted, for they obviously know no other.

The real weakness of the old local color fiction of the 1880–1910 era derived from its condescending attitude toward the regional characteristics that the author undertook to exploit. The local colorist played up what would appear quaint or funny or at any rate outlandish. He was the spielman for a rubberneck bus taking tourists through the hinterland. His job was to amuse the sophisticated by exhibiting the antics of the natives. In short, he could not afford to take his characters seriously as human beings in their own right. James Still does not make this mistake.

Speaking for the moment personally, I was born in Kentucky and lived there during some highly impressionable years. My home was in the western tip of the state, about as far from James Still's mountains as a fellow Kentuckian could get. Yet many of the customs, superstitions, and folkways that Still mentions are familiar to me. I have seen a person "walk his chair" across a room. (By shifting your weight you can teeter a straight chair—not a rocker—across the floor without ever completely rising from it.) I learned to blow soap bubbles by using a discarded spool as a blowpipe just as children on Troublesome Creek do. As a boy I learned to "rooster fight." "Hollow tail," that mythical disease afflicting milch cattle, was diagnosed in one of my father's cows. The "dumb bull," described in the story "On Quicksand Creek," was new to me, but I had heard of the "tick tack," that minor instrument of the devil which could be used to scare a cantankerous neighbor.

The stories in this volume are indeed stories, with simple but adequate plots, a due measure of suspense, and an interesting variety of characters. In those stories narrated by the boy, things, good and bad, happen to his family and happen to the boy as he grows toward an adult's possession of his world. These stories thus make up a modest *Bildungsroman,* a mode that has clearly provided some of the best fiction in the whole range of American literature. One thinks immediately of Twain's Huck Finn, or Hemingway's Nick Adams, or Faulkner's young isaac McCaslin, or Sherwood Anderson's Kentucky boy who is the narrator of "I Want to Know Why." Still has made a worthy contribution to this genre.

It is sheer gain, then, to have the stories in *The Run for the Elbertas* now available in this one volume. They need not merely to be preserved as an item in our literary history, but made accessible to the reading public as a piece of living literature.

CLEANTH BROOKS

*That was their way. Lonely folk, but a blessing to each other, for the beasts, and for the earth.*

Knut Hamsun, *Growth of the Soil*

# I Love My Rooster

WE lived in Houndshell mine camp the year of the coal boom, and I remember the mines worked three shifts a day. The conveyors barely ceased their rusty groaning for five months. I recollect the plenty there was, and the silver dollars rattling wherever men walked; and I recollect the goldfinches stayed that winter through, their yellow breasts turning mole-gray.

We were eating supper on a November evening when Sim Brannon, the foreman, came to tell Father of the boom. Word came that sudden. Father talked alone with Sim in the front room, coming back to the kitchen after a spell. A chuckle of joy broke in his throat as he sat down at the table again, swinging the baby off the floor onto his knee. He reached for the bowl of shucky beans, shaping a hill of them on his plate with a spoon. Never had he let us play with victuals. "They've tuck the peg off o' coal," he said. "Government's pulled the price tag. Coal will be selling hand over fist."

The baby stuck a finger into the bean mound. Father didn't scold. Mother lifted the coffeepot, shaking the spout clear of grounds. "I never heard tell it had a peg," she said.

Fern and Lark and I looked at Father, wondering what a coal peg was. The baby's face was bright and wise, as if he knew.

Father thumped the table, marking his words. "I say it's ontelling what a ton o' coal will sell for. They's a lack afar north at the big lakes, and in countries across the waters. I figure the price will double or treble." He lifted a hand over the baby's head. "Yon blue sky might be the limit."

Our heads turned toward the window. We saw only the night sky, dark as gob smoke.

Mother set the coffeepot down, for it began to tremble in her hand. She thrust a stick of wood into the stove, though supper was done and the room warm. "Will there be plenty in the camps?" she asked, uncertain.

Father laughed, spoon in air. "Best times ever hit this country," he said, jarring the table. "Why, I'm a-liable to draw twice the pay I get now." He paused, staring at us. We sat as under a charm, listening. "We're going to feed these chaps till they're fat as mud," he went on. "Going to put proper clothes on their backs and buy them a few pretties. We'll live like folks were born to live. This hardscrabble skimping I'm tired of. We're going to fare well."

The baby made a cluck with his tongue, trying to talk. He squeezed a handful of beans until they popped between his fingers.

"For one thing," Father said, "I'm going to buy me a pair o' high-top boots. These clodhoppers I'm wearing have wore a half acre o' bark off my heels."

The cracked lids of the stove began to wink. Heat grew in the room.

"I want me a fact'ry dress," Fern spoke.

"I need me a shirt," I said. "A boughten shirt. And I want a game rooster. One that'll stand on my shoulder and crow."

Father glanced at me, suddenly angry.

"Me," Lark began, "I want—" But he could not think what he wanted most of all.

"A game rooster!" Father exclaimed. "They's too many gamble cocks in this camp already. Why, I'd a'soon buy you a pair o' dice and a card deck. I'd a'soon."

"A pet rooster wouldn't harm a hair," I said, the words small and stubborn in my throat. And I thought of one-eyed Fedder Mott, who oft played mumbly-peg with me, and who went to the rooster matches at the Hack. Fedder would tell of the fights, his eye patch shaking, and I would wonder what there was behind the patch. I'd always longed to spy.

"No harm, as I see, in a pet chicken," Mother said.

"I want me a banty," Lark said.

Father grinned, his anger gone. He batted an eye at Mother. "We hain't going into the fowl business," he said. "That's for shore." He gave the baby a spoonful of beans. "While ago I smelled fish on Sim Brannon—fried salt fish he'd just et for supper. I'm a-mind to buy a whole wooden kit o' mackerel. We'll be able."

Mother raised the window a grain, yet it seemed no less hot. She sat down at the foot of the table. The baby jumped on Father's knee, reaching arms toward her. His lips rounded, quivering to speak. A bird sound came out of his mouth.

"I bet he wants a pretty-piece bought for him," Fern said.

"By juckers," Father said, "if they was a trinket would larn him to talk, I'd buy it." He balanced the baby in the palm of a hand and held him straight out, showing his strength. Then he keened his eyes at Mother. "You hain't said what you want. All's had their say except you."

Mother stared into her plate. She studied the wedge print there. She did not lift her eyes.

"Come riddle, come riddle," Father said impatiently.

"The thing I want hain't a sudden idea," Mother said quietly. Her voice seemed to come from a long way off. "My notion has followed me through all the coal camps we've lived in, a season here, a span there, forever moving. Allus I've aimed to have a house built on the acres we heired on Shoal Creek o' Troublesome. Fifteen square acres we'd have to raise our chaps proper. Garden patches to grow victuals. Elbowroom a-plenty. Fair times and bad, we'd have a roof-tree. Now, could we save half you make, we'd have enough money in time."

"Half?" Father questioned. "Why, we're going to start living like folks. Fitten clothes on our backs, food a body can enjoy." He shucked his coat, for he sat nearest the stove. He wiped sweat beads off his forehead.

"I need me a shirt," I said. "A store-bought shirt." More

than a game rooster, more than anything, I wanted a shirt
made like a man's. Being eight years old, I was ashamed to
wear the ones Mother sewed without tails to stuff inside my
breeches.

"No use living barebones in the midst o' plenty," Father
said. "Half is too much."

Mother rose from the table and leaned over the stove. She
looked inside to see if anything had been left to burn. She
tilted the coffeepot, making sure it hadn't boiled dry. "Where
there's a boom one place," she said, "there's bound to be a
famine in another. Coal gone high, and folks not able to
pay." Her lips trembled. "Fires gone out. Chaps chill and sick
the world over withouten a roof above their heads." She
picked up the poker, lifted a stove cap, and shook the embers.
Drops of water began to fry on the stove. She was crying.

"Be-grabbies!" Father said. "Stop poking that fire! This
room's already hot as a ginger mill."


On a Saturday afternoon Father brought his two-week
pay pocket home, the first since the boom. He came into the
kitchen, holding it aloft, unopened. Mother was cooking a
skillet of meal mush and the air was heavy with the good
smell. I was in haste to eat and go, having promised Fedder
Mott to meet him at the schoolhouse gate. Fedder and I
planned to climb the mine tipple.

"Corn in the hopper and meal in the sack," Father said,
rattling the pocket.

He let Fern and Lark push fingers against it, feeling the
greenbacks inside; and he gave it to the baby to play with
upon the floor, watching out of the tail of his eye. Mother
was uneasy with Father's carelessness. The baby opened his
mouth, clucking, churring. He made a sound like a wren
setting a nest of eggs.

"Money, money," Fern said, trying to teach him.

He twisted his lips, his tongue straining. But he could not
speak a word.

"I'd give every red cent to hear him say one thing," Father said.

The pay pocket was opened, the greenbacks spread upon the table. We had never seen such a bounty. Father began to figure slowly with fingers and lips. Fern counted swiftly. She could count nearly as fast as the Houndshell schoolteacher.

Father paused, watching Fern. "This chap can out-count a check-weigh-man," he bragged.

"Sixty-two dollars and thirty cents," Fern announced, and it was right, for Mother had counted too. "Wisht I had me a fact'ry dress," Fern said.

"I want a shirt hain't allus a-gaping at the top o' my breeches," I said.

Father wrinkled his forehead. "These chaps need clothes, I reckon. And I've got my fancy set on a pair o' boots. They's no use going about like raggle-taggle gypsies with money in hand. We're able to live decent."

"Socks and stockings I've knit," Mother said, "and shirts and dress garments I've sewed a-plenty for winter. They hain't made by store pattern, but they'll wear and keep a body warm. Now, I'm willing to do without and live hard to build a homeplace."

"Oh, I'm willing, too," Father complained, "but a man likes to get his grunt and groan in." He gathered the greenbacks, handing them to Mother. He stacked the three dimes. "Now, if I wasn't allus seeing the money, I could save without hurt. Once hit touches my sight and pocket, I'm afire. I burn to spend."

Mother rolled the bills. She thrust them into an empty draw sack, stowing all in her bosom. "One thing you could do," she told Father, "but it's not for me to say do, or not do. If you was a-mind, you could bring the pay pockets home unopened. We'd not think to save just half. I'd save all we could bear, spend what was needed. You'd not see the spark of a dime till we got enough for a house. I say this boom can't last eternal."

Father pulled his eyebrows, deciding. The baby watched.

How like a bird he cocked his head. "Oh, I'm a-mind," Father said at last, "but the children ought to have a few coins to pleasure themselves with. A nickel a week."

"I want mine broke in pennies," Lark called.

Fern counted swiftly, speaking in dismay, "It would take me nigh a year to save enough for an ordered dress."

"We'll not lack comfort nor pleasure," Mother promised. "Nor will we waste. The chaps can have the nickel. You get a pair o' boots—a pair not too costy. And we'll buy a kit o' fish."

She stirred butter into the meal mush, and it was done. Fern hurried dishes upon the table.

"The pair my head was set on cost eighteen dollars. Got toes so sharp you could kick a blacksnake's eye out. Reckon I'll just make these clodbusters I got on do."

"Them boots must o' been sprigged with gold tacks."

A buttery steam rose from our plates. We dipped up spoonfuls of mush; we scraped our dishes, pushing them back for more.

"Hit's good to see no biled leather breeches on the table for once," Father said. He blew on a spoon of mush to cool it for the baby. "Right today I'll buy that kit o' fish."

"They're liable to draw every cat in Houndshell Holler. Better you plug the cat hole in the back door first."

I slid from the table bench, pulling my hat off a peg.

"Where are you traipsing to?" Father asked.

"Going to play with Fedder Mott. He's yonder in the schoolyard."

"I know Fedder Mott," Lark spoke, gulping much. "He's a boy jist got one eyeball."

I ran the Houndshell road. A banjo twanged among the houses. A hundred smokes stirred in chimney pots, rising, threading chilly air. I reached the schoolhouse, breathing hard, and Fedder Mott was swinging on the gate. He jumped down.

"I'd nigh give you out," he said, his blue eye wide.

I said, "If my pap knowed about the tipple, I'd not got to come."

Fedder leaned against the fence. He was a full head taller than I, a year older. He drew a whack of tobacco from a hind pocket, bit a squirrely bite, and offered the cut to me.

I shook my head.

He puckered his lips, speaking around the wad in his jaw. "They hain't nothing worth seeing in that tipple tower. I done climbed thar." He waited, champing teeth into the wad, making juice to spit. "I'd figured we'd go to the rooster fight. Now you've come too late."

"Was I to go," I said, "my pap would tear up stakes."

Two children ran by, playing tag-o. A man came walking the road. Fedder spat into a rut. The black patch trembled on his face. It was like a great dark eye, dwarfing the blue one. I looked at it curiously.

"Afore long, fellers will be coming down from the Hack," Fedder said. "We'll larn which roosters whooped."

I studied the eye patch. It was the size of a silver dollar, hanging by a string looped around his head. What lay behind it? Was there a hole square into his skull? I was almost ashamed to ask, almost afraid. I drew a circle on the ground with my shoe toe, measuring the words: "I'll go to the rooster fight sometime, if one thing—"

"If'n what?"

"If you'll let me see your eye pocket."

Fedder blew the tobacco cud across the road. He pushed the long tails of his shirt inside his breeches. "You'll spy and won't go."

" 'F'ad die."

We saw a man walking the path off the ridge, coming toward us from the Hack. He came fast, though he was still too distant to be named. We watched him wind the crooked path and be lost among the houses.

"Ag'in' we go to the cockpit," Fedder said, "I'll let you look."

"I choose now."

Fedder stood firm. "Ag'in' that time, I will." He hushed a moment, listening for the man who came from the ridge. "Afore long I'll not be wearing this patch," he said. "I've heared o' glass eyeballs. Hit's truth. They say even a hound dog wears one in Anvers camp. Five round dollars they cost, and could I grab a holt on that much, I'd git the schoolteacher to mail an order."

"Won't your pap buy you a glass 'un?"

"If'n I was a flycatcher, he wouldn't feed me gnats."

"I'm going to save money, come every week. I've got me something in my head to buy."

"Hit reads in a magazine where a feller kin sell garden seeds and make a profit. A hundred packages o' squash and dill and turnip sold, and I'd have me enough."

We saw the man afar off on the road. He was heading our way, walking a hippety-hop on short legs.

"Bulger Hyden," Fedder said.

Fedder hailed him as he reached the schoolhouse gate, and he stopped. He shed his coat, being warm from haste, and he wore a green-dotted shirt.

"Who whooped?" Fedder asked.

Bulger Hyden's face grew wrinkled as a doty mushroom; he swung his arms emptily, glancing at the sky's promise of weather. There was a hint of snow. Goldfinches blew over us like leaves, piping their dry winter song above the conveyor's ceaseless rattle.

"Steph Harben's Red Pyle rimwrecked my Duckwing," Bulger grumbled. "Steph fotched that bird from West Virginia and scratches in all the money. I say it hain't fair pitting a furren cock." He folded his coat, balancing it on an elbow crotch, making ready to go. "I thought a sight o' my little Duckwing." His voice hoarsened. "I cherished that rooster." And he went on, and I looked after him, thinking a green-speckled shirt was the choicest garment ever a fellow could wear.

Winter came before I could go to the Hack. Snow fell late in November and scarcely left the ground for two months. The rooster fights were halted until spring. I recollect the living river of wind pouring down Houndshell Hollow. For bird and varmint, and, I hear, for folk beyond the camps, it was a lean time. But miners fared well. I recollect the warm linsey coats, the red woolen gloves, the high-top boots; I recollect full pokes of food going into houses, and the smell of cooking victuals. Children wore store clothes. They bought spin-tops and pretties at the commissary. Boys' pockets clinked money. Only Fedder Mott and I had to wind our own balls and whittle our tops. I hoarded the nickels Mother gave me, telling Fedder I might buy a shirt when enough had been saved. Fedder never had a penny. He spoke bitterly of it. "My pap wouldn't plait me shucks if'n I was a chair bottom." And he said, "I hear tell hit's might' nigh the same with yore pap. Hit's told the eagle squalls when he looses a dollar."

Mother spent little. We hardly dared complain, having already more than we had known before. Once, in January, Father tried to figure the amount of money Mother had stored in the draw sack. He marked with a stub pencil, and Mother watched. At last he let the baby have the pencil. "My wage has riz three times," he said hopelessly, "though I don't know how much. Why, fellers tell me they're getting twelve and fifteen dollars a day. Deat Sheldon claims he made twenty dollars, four days handrunning, but he works a fold in the gravy tunnel and can load standing up."

"I've no idea o' the sum we've got," Mother said. "I opened one pay pocket and we're living out of it. The rest I've kept sealed."

"How's a body to know when a plenty's been saved? I hain't in a notion yet setting aside for tombstone and coffin box. Fellers in the mines 'gin to say the buffalo bellows when I spend a nickel."

"If you long for a thing enough, you'll give up for it. You'll sacrifice. The coal famine is bound to end some day.

Come that time, we'll fit the house to the money."

Father began to tease. "What say we count the greenbacks? My curiosity is being et raw."

"Now, no. Hit would be a temptation to spend."

The baby sat up, threshing the air, puckering his lips. We looked, and he had bitten the rubber tip off the pencil.

"Hain't he old enough to be saying words?" Father asked.

"He talked to a cat once," Lark said. "I heared him."

"Ah, now," Mother chided. "Just a sound he made. Cats follow stealing in since we bought salt fish. Can't keep the cat hole plugged."

"He said 'kigid.'"

"That hain't a word," Fern said.

Father poked a finger at the baby. "By gollyard, if he'd just speak one word!"

The baby lifted his arms, mouth wide, neck stretched. He crowed.

"Thar's your rooster," Father chuckled, setting his eyes on me.

"I aim to own a real gamer," I bragged, irked by Father's teasing. "I aim to." I spoke without hope, not knowing that by spring it would come true.

"A good thing to have this double zero weather," Father drawled. "Hit driv the poker players and fowl gamblers indoors. But fellers claim that when the weather mends they'll be rooster fights in the Hack three days a week. Hit's high-low-jack and them fools lose every button cent."

Mother searched the baby's mouth for the pencil tip. "I call this boom a gamble," she said. "It's bound to end." She didn't find the rubber tip, for the baby had swallowed it down.

I told Fedder of Mother's prophecy as we sat by a fire on the creek bank. We had fish-hooks in an ice hole.

"Be-hopes the boom lasts till I git me a glass eye," he said. "My mind's set on it. I'd better have a batch o' garden seeds ordered and start selling."

"You couldn't stick a pickax in the ground, it's so froze," I told him. "Folks haven't a notion to buy seeds now."

Fedder rubbed his hands over the blaze, blowing a foggy breath. "I say winter hain't going to last forever neither."

I recollect thinking the long cold spell would never end. January diddled, and February crawled. March warmed a bit, thawing. The breasts of goldfinches turned yellow as rubbed gold again. Fedder got his seeds, though when he should have been peddling them he'd climb the ridge to the rooster fights. Oft when a rooster was killed they'd let him bring the dead fowl home. Father forbade my going to the Hack; he put his foot down. But next to seeing was Fedder's telling. I came to know the names of the bravest cocks. I knew their markings, and the way they fought.

Fedder whistled for me one Thursday evening at the edge of dark. I heard and went outside, knowing his Kentucky redbird call. He stood beyond the fence with a coffee sack bundled in his arms; and he seemed fearful and anxious, and yet proud. His blue eye was wide, and the black patch had a living look. Packages of seeds rattled in his pockets.

"How much money have you mized?" he asked. "How much?" His voice was a husky whisper.

I guessed what the bundle held, scarcely daring to believe. I grew feverish with wonder.

"Eleven nickels," I said. "I couldn't save all."

The coffee sack moved; something threshed inside. A fowl's wings struck its thighs.

"I'm a-mind to sell you half ownership in my rooster," he said. "I will for yore eleven nickels, and if you'll keep him till I find a place. My pap would wring hits neck if I tuck him home."

I touched the bundle. My hand trembled. I shook with joy. "I been saving to buy a shirt," I said. "I want me a boughten shirt."

"You couldn't save enough by Kingdom Come. Eleven nickels, and jist you pen him. We'll halvers."

"Who'd he belong to?"

"Fotch the money. All's got to be helt a secret."

I brought my tobacco-sack bank and Father's mine lamp. We stole under the house, penning the rooster in a hen-coop. Father's voice droned over us in the kitchen. Fedder lit the lamp to count the money. The rooster stood blinking, red-eyed, alert. His shoulders were white, redding at the wing bows. Blood beads tipped his hackle feathers. His spurs were trimmed to fit gaffs. It was Steph Harben's Red Pyle.

"How'd you come by him?" I insisted.

"He fit Ebo, the black Cuban, and got stumped. He keeled down. They was a cut on his throat and you'd a-thought him knob dead. Steph give him to me, and ere I reached the camp, he come alive. That thar cut was jist a scratch."

We crawled from beneath the house. Fedder smothered the light. "Don't breathe this to a soul," he warned. "Steph would auger to git him back, and my pap would throw duck fits. Now, you bring him to the schoolhouse ag'in' two o'clock tomorrow."

He moved toward the gate, the nickels ringing in his pocket. I went into the house and sat quietly behind the stove, feeling lost without my money, though recompensed by the rooster.

Father spoke, trotting the baby to Burnham Bright on a foot. "Warm weather's come," he mused. "Seems to me the Houndshell company ought to pare down on mining. Two days ago they hired four new miners, fellers from away yander."

"I know a boy come from Alabamy," Lark said. "I bet he's from yon side the waters."

"It's United States, America," Fern said.

"Sim Brannon believes something's bound to crack before long," Father went on. "Says hit's liable to come sudden. I'm in hopes my job don't split off."

"Come that time," Mother said, "maybe we'll have plenty saved for a house."

Father reached the baby to Mother. "I'm going to bed early," he yawned. "Last night I never got sixty winkles o' sleep. I reckon every tomcat in this camp was miaowing on the back porch."

"The fish draws 'um."

"A tinker man tapped on the door yesterday," Fern said, "and a big nanny cat ran in betwixt his legs."

"Hit's the one baby talked a word to," Lark said.

Father stretched sleepily. "I'm afeared the baby's a mute," he said. He set his chair aside. "The only thing that'd keep me awake this night would be counting the money we've got stacked away."


I waited at the schoolhouse gate, holding the rooster by the shanks. He snuggled against my jump jacket, pecking at the buttons. He stuck his head in my jacket pocket to see what was there. After a spell Fedder came, his eye patch trembling and the garden seeds as noisy upon him as grass crickets.

"Why'n't you kiver him?" he asked crossly. "He might a-been seen."

"He flopped the coffee sack off," I said. "Anyhow, he's been seen already. Crowed this morning before blue daylight and woke my pap. If I hadn't cried like gall, he'd been killed. Now it's your turn to keep."

Fedder bit a chew of tobacco, bit it with long front teeth as a squirrel bites. He spat into the road and looked up and down. "If I tuck him to my house, he'd be in the skillet by dinner." He closed his eye to think, and there was only the black patch staring. "I figure Steph Harben will buy him back. He's yon side the commissary, playing draughts. Air you of a notion?"

The cock lifted his head, poising it left and right. I loosed my hold about his legs and stroked his bright saddle. He sat on my arm.

"This rooster's a pet," I said. "When I tuck him out o' the

coop, he jumped square onto my shoulder and crowed. I'm taking a liking to him."

"I jist lack selling fourteen seed papers gitting my eyeball. Never could I sell dills and rutabagas. If Steph will buy the rest, I'll rid my part. We got nowheres earthy to store a chicken."

"I hain't a-mind to sell."

Fedder packed the ground where he stood. The seeds rattled. The rooster pricked his head.

"You stay here till I git Steph," Fedder said. He swung around. "You stay."

He went in haste, and suddenly a great silence fell in the camp. The coal conveyor at the mines had stopped. Men stood at the drift mouth and looked down upon the rooftops. It was so still I could hear the far *per-chic-o-ree* of finches. I held the rooster at arm's length, wishing him free as a bird. I half hoped he would fly away. I set him on the fence, but he hopped to my shoulder and shook his wattles.

Back along the road came Fedder. Steph Harben hastened with him, wearing a shirt like striped candy, and never a man wore a finer one. The shirt was thinny—so thin that when he stood before me I could see the paddles of his collarbones.

Fedder said, "I've sold my part. Hit's you two trading."

Steph said, "Name yore price. Name."

I gathered the fowl in my arms. "I hain't a-mind to sell," I said.

We turned to stare at miners passing, going home long before quitting time, their cap lamps burning in broad day.

Steph was anxious. "Why hain't you willing?" he asked. "Name."

I dug my toe into the ground, scuffing dirt. "I love my rooster," I said. But I looked at Steph's shirt. It was very beautiful.

"If'n you'll sell," Fedder promised, "I'll let you spy at my eye pocket. Now, while it's thar, you kin look. Afore long I'll have a glass 'un."

I kicked a clod into the road. "I'll swap my part o' the rooster for that striped shirt. It can be cut down to fit."

"Shuck it off," Fedder told Steph.

Steph unbuttoned the shirt, slipped it over the blades of his shoulders, and handed it to me in a wad. He snatched the rooster, lighting out for home, and miners along the road glared at his bare back.

Fedder brushed his hat aside, catching the eye patch between forefinger and thumb. I was suddenly afraid, suddenly having no wish to see.

The patch was lifted. I looked, stepping back, squeezing the shirt into a ball. I turned, running, running with this sight burnt upon my mind.

I ran all the way home, going into the kitchen door as Father went, not staying the sow cat that stole in between my legs. Mother sat at the table, a pile of greenbacks before her, the empty pay pockets crumpled.

"Hell's bangers!" Father gasped, dropping heavily upon a chair and lifting the baby to his knee; and when he could speak above his wonder, "The boom's busted. I've got no job." But he laughed, and Mother smiled.

"I've heard already," Mother said. She laid a hand upon the money bills, flicking them under a thumb like a deck of gamble cards. "There's enough here to build a house, a house with windows looking out o' every room. And a grain left for a pair o' costy boots, a boughten shirt, a fact'ry dress, a few pretties."

The baby opened his mouth, curling his lips, pointing a stub finger. He pointed at the old nanny smelling the fish kit.

"Cat!" he said, big as life.

# The Proud Walkers

*W*E moved out of Houndshell mine camp in May to the homeplace Father had built on Shoal Creek, and I recollect foxgrapes were blooming and there was a spring chill in the air. Fern and Lark and I ran ahead of the wagon, frightening water thrushes, shouting back at the poky mare. We broke cowcumber branches to wave at the baby, wanting to call to him, but he did not then have a name.

Only Mother forbore stretching eyes to see afar. She held the baby atop a shuck tick, her face pale with dread to look upon the house. A mort of things she had told Father before he had gone to raise the dwelling. "Ere a board is rived," she'd said, "dig a cellar. There'll be no more pokes o' victuals coming from the commissary." She had told him the pattern for the chimney, roof, and walls; she told him more than a body could keep in his head, saying at last, "Could I lend a hand, 'twould be a satisfaction."

Father had grinned. "A nail you drove would turn corkscrew. A blow-sarpent couldn't quile to your saw marks. Hit's man's work. A man's got to wear the breeches." Oh, Father nearly had a laughing spell listening to Mother's talk. Mother had said, "A house proper to raise chaps in, a cellar for laying by food, and lasty neighbors. Now, that hain't asking for the moon-ball."

I recollect bull-bats soared overhead when we reached Shoal Creek in the late afternoon; I recollect Mother looked at the house, and all she had feared was true. The building stood windowless, board ends of walls were unsawn, and the chimney pot barely cleared the hip-roof. But Fern and Lark and I were awed. We could not think why Mother dabbed her eyes with baby's dress tail.

"Hit's not finished to a square T," Father said uneasily. "After planting they'll be time in plenty. A late start I've got. Why, field corn and a garden ought to be breaking ground. Just taste a grain o' patience."

Mother glanced into the sky where bull-bats hawked. She was heartsick with the mulligrubs. Her voice sounded tight and strange. "A man's notions are ontelling," she said, "but if this creek's a fitten place to bring up chaps, if good neighbors live nigh, reckon I've got no right to complain."

"The Crownover family lives yon side the ridge," Father said. "Only folks in handy walking distance. I hear they're the earth's salt. No needcessity o' lock or key on Shoal Creek."

The wagon was unloaded by dusk dark. Father lighted the lamp on coming from stabling the mare, and we hovered to a smidgen of fire. We trembled in the night chill, for it was foxgrape winter. Mother feared to heap wood on the blaze, the chimney pot being low enough to set sparks to the roof. She knelt by the hearth, frying a skillet of hominy, cooking it mortal slow.

Father saddled the baby on a knee. "Well, now," he said, buttoning his jump jacket and peeping to see what the skillet held, "reckon I've caught a glimpse o' neighbors already. I heard footsteps yon side the barn in a brushy draw, though I couldn't see for blackness till they'd topped the ridge. There walked two fellers, with heads size o' washpots."

Lark crept nearer Mother. Fern and I glanced behind us. Nailheads shone on the walls as bright as the eyes of beasts.

"I figure it to be men carrying churns or jugs on their shoulders," Mother spoke coldly.

"I saw a water-head baby in the camps once," Fern said. "I did."

"Hit might a-been Old Bloody Tom and some'un," Lark said.

"Odd they'd go by our place," Father mused, "traveling

no path." He joggled the baby on his knee, making him squeal. "But it's said them Crownovers can be trusted to Jordan River and back ag'in. I'm wanting to get acquainted the first chance."

"A man's fancy to take short cuts," Mother replied, nodding her head at the boxed room. "They're men cutting across from one place to another, taking the lazy trail."

Fern's teeth chattered. She was ever the scary one.

"I hain't a chip afraid," I bragged, rashy with curiosity. "Be they boys amongst them Crownovers? I'm a-mind to play with one."

"Gee-o," Father chuckled, "a whole bee swarm o' chaps. Stair-steppers, creepers, and climbers, biddy ones to nigh growns. Fourteen, by honest count. A sawyer at Beddo Tillett's mill says they all can whoop weeds out of a crop in one day."

"I be not to play with water-heads," Lark said.

"That sawyer says every one o' Izard Crownover's young 'uns have rhymy names," Father went on. "He spun me a few, many as he could think of. Bard, Nard, Dard, Guard, Shard—names so slick yore tongue trips up."

"Are there girls too?" Fern asked.

"Beulah, Dulah, Eulah. A string like that."

Mother stirred the hominy. "Clever neighbors I've allus wanted," she said, her voice gloomy, "and allus I've longed for a house fitten to make them welcome."

"Be-jibs!" Father spoke impatiently. "A fair homeseat we'll have once the crop's planted, and they's a spare minute. Why, I raised this place off the ground in twelve days, elbow for axle. I didn't have half the proper tools; I had no help-hands. I hauled lumber twelve miles from Beddo Tillett's sawmill." He grunted, untangling baby's fingers from his watch chain. "Anyhow, hit might take them Crownovers a year's thawing to visit. Hain't like the camps where folks stick noses in, the first thing. I say let time get in its lick."

We were quieted by the thought of enduring a lonesome year, of nobody coming to put his feet under our table, nobody to borrow, or heave and set and calculate weather. Oh, the camps had spoiled us with their slew of chaps and rattling coal conveyors and people's talky-talk. Dwelling there, you couldn't stretch your elbows without hitting people.

I said, sticking my lips out, "I hain't waiting till I'm crook-back ere I play with some'un."

Fern batted her eyes, trying to cry. "Ruther to live on a gob heap than where no girls are."

The skillet jiggled in Mother's hand. She spoke, complaining of the house, though now it was small in her mind compared with this new anxiety. "Nary a window cut," she said. "A house blind as a mole varmint."

"Jonah's whale!" Father exclaimed angrily. His ears reddened. He galloped his knee. "A feller can't whittle window-frames with a pocket knife. I reckon nothing will do but I hie at daybreak to Tillett's and 'gin making them. Two days it'll take; two I ought to be rattling clods. Why, a week's grubbing to be done before a furrow's lined. Crops won't mature planted so late." He swallowed a great breath. "Had we the finest cellar in Amerikee, a particle o' nothing there'd be for winter storing."

"I reckon I've set my bonnet too high," Mother admitted. "The cellar's got to be filled with canning, turnips, cabbages, and pickling, if we're to eat the year through. Now, windows can be put off, but the chimley's bound to have a taller stacking."

The blood hasted from Father's ears. Never could he stay angry long. He coaxed baby to latch hands on his lifted arm and swing. "Ought to fill the new barn loft so full o' corn and fodder hits tongue will hang out," he said. He taught the baby to skin a cat, come-Andy-over, head foremost. "One thing besides frames I'm fotching, and that's a name for this tadwhacker. Long enough he's gone without."

"Hain't going to call him Beddo," Fern said. "That's the ugliest name-word ever was."

"Not to be Tillett neither," Lark said.

The hominy browned. We held plates in our laps. The

yellow kernels steamed a mellow smell. It was hard not to gobble them down like an old craney crow.

Mother ate a bit, then sat watching Father. "I had a house pattern in my head," she said, "and I ached to help build, to try my hand making it according. And I'd wished for good neighbors. But house and neighbors hain't a circumstance to getting a crop and the garden planted. Hit's back to the mines for us if we don't make victuals. Them windowframes can wait."

"I can't follow a woman's notions," Father said. "For peace o' mind I'd better gamble two days and get the windows in." He chuckled, his mouth crammed. "I'd give a Tennessee pearl to see you atop a twenty-foot ladder potting nails." His chuckle grew to laughter; it caught like a wind in his chest, blowing out in gusts, shaking him. He began to cough. A kernel had got in his windpipe. His jaws turned beety; he sneezed a great sneeze. We struck our doubled fists against his back, and presently the grain was dislodged. "Ah, ho," he said, swallowing, "had I a-died, 'twould been in good cause."

Mother lightened. "I'm no witty with a hammer and saw," she said, "and if that cellar's not dug to my fancy, I can spade."

Father sobered. He got as restless in his chair as a caged bird. Of a sudden he turned his head to the door, listening. "Hush-o!" he said. We pricked our ears. "Hush!"

We waited, unbreathing, hearing the harsh *peent* of bull-bats.

"I heard nothing onnatural," Mother said.

Fern shivered. Lark searched under the beds. He knew boogers were abroad at night.

Father reached the baby to Mother, and got up. So sleepy baby was, his head rolled like a dropped gourd. "The mare's restless," Father decided. "She might o' heard Crownover's stally bray yon side the mountain. I'll see that she's latched in tight." He went outside.

"Let's play Old Bloody Tom," Lark said. "I be Tom, a-rambling, smoking my pipe. You all be sheeps."

"Now, no," Fern snuffed. "It'd make me scared."

We children were abed when Father returned. He shucked off his boots and dabbed tallow on them; he breathed on the leather and rubbed it fiercely with a linsey rag. He spoke, faltering, hunting words, "I've been aiming to tell about the cellar."

Mother fitted a skillet's eye to a peg. She paused.

"After I'd shingled the roof," Father said, "I put in to dig. Got three feet down and struck bottom. This house is setting on living rock. I've larnt they hain't a cellar on Shoal Creek. This vein runs under all."

And later, when the light was blown, I heard Father speak from his pillow. "I saw more fellers on the ridge a while ago, walking with heads so square I figured they hefted boxes on their shoulders. I'm a-mind to stop by the Crownovers' to-morrow, asking a hinting question. Hit's quare folks would go a dark way no road treads."

The sun-ball was eating creek fog when Mother waked me. The door stood wide upon morning. "Your father's gone to Tillett's already," she said, "and against my will and beg. He hurried off afoot, saying he'd let the mare rest, saying he'd get the windowframes hauled somehow." She gazed dole-somely upon the fields where blackgum, sassafras, and red-bud grew as in a young forest. "I argued, I plead, yet he would to go. Oh, man-judgment's like weather. Hit's onknowing."

My breeches were on in a wink. I'd thought to go feed the mare, then hie to the brushy draw to quest for signs of walk-ers. I went before eating, being more curious than hungry. I fed the mare ten ears of corn; I stole beyond the barn. The draw was a moggy place. Wahoos grew thick against a limerock wall, and a sprangle of water ran out. I found a nest of brogan tracks set in the mud; I saw where they printed the ridge. "If I was growed up," I spoke aloud, "I'd follow them steps, be they go to the world's end." Then I ran to the house; I ran so fast a bluesnake racer couldn't have caught me.

Mother was putting dough bread and rashers on the table when I hurried indoors. Her face was gaunt with worry. She circled the table where Fern and Lark ate. Baby threshed in his tall chair, sucking a meat rind. "It would take Adam's grands and greats to rid that ground in time for planting," she said. "I tried grubbing a pawpaw, but its roots sunk to Chiney. I'm afeared we might have to backtrack to the mines. We'll be bound to, if the crops don't bear."

"I've seen a quare thing," I said.

Mother paid me no mind. "Two days your father will be gone, and no satisfaction I'll see till he returns. Yet he can't grub by his lone. He'd not get through in time." She halted, staring at the walls, searching in her head for what to do.

"Never was a mine shack darker," she said at last, having decided. She rolled her sleeves above her elbows, like a man's. "I can't grub fitten. I can't dig a cellar through puore rock. But window holes I can saw—holes three feet by five." She fetched a hatchet and a handsaw; she marked a window by tape.

"I'd be scared of a night, with holes cut," Fern complained. "Robber men might come."

"I saw tracks," I blurted. My words were drowned under Mother's chopping. She hewed a crevice to give the sawblade lee.

"It's Father's work," Fern whined. She squeezed her eyelids, trying to cry.

I recollect Mother worked that day through, cutting four windows, true as a sawyer's. The hours crawled turkle-slow. Fern and Lark and I longed for shouting children; we longed for the busy noises of the camps. We could only mope and look at the empty road. Nobody passed up-creek or down, nobody we glimpsed from daybreak to dusk dark. Oft when Mother took a little rest she'd glance the hills over. Oh, she was lost as anyone. Loneliness swelled large as mast-balls inside of us.

When night came we heard the first lorn cry of a chuck-will's-widow. The evening chill was sharp. We ate supper huddled to a mite of fire. "One spark against a shingle," Mother explained, "and we'd have to roust a fox from his cave house. That chimley begs fixing."

The dishes were washed and put away. We sat quietly, our faces yellow in the lamplight. The *peent* of bull-bats came through the window holes. Spring lizards prayed for rain in the bottoms.

Mother saw how our eyes kept stealing to the window. The darkness there was black as corpse cloth. "Sing a ballad or play a game," she urged. "Then hap baby will go to sleep."

"Play Bloody Tom," Lark called. "I be Tom, coming for a coal to tetch my pipe. You be sheeps or chaps."

"Now, no," Fern said, "that 'un's scary."

"Let's do a talking song," I chose. "Let's sing 'Old Rachel,' and me do the talking."

We sang "Old Rachel"; Old Rachel nobody could do a thing with; Old Rachel going to the Bad Place with her toenails dragging and a bucket on her arm, saying, "Good morning, Mister Devil, hit's getting mighty warm"; and I spoke, after every verse, "Now, listen, Little Rachel, please be kind o' quiet."

We hushed suddenly. Beast sounds rang the hills. Crown-over's stallion had trumpeted afar, and our mare had whinnied.

"Sing ahead," Mother coaxed, "the mare's stall is latched. I saw to it. Sing what the Devil done with Rachel when he couldn't handle her."

We had no heart to sing more. "I propped the stall door," I said. Fern's eyes were beaded upon the black window. "Wisht it was allus day," she said.

"Ah, now," Mother chided, trying to comfort us. "A body gets their growth of a night. I'd not want the baby a dwarf."

"I saw a low-standing man in the camps once," Fern recalled, "not nigh tall as me."

"I saw tracks in the draw—" I began, and hushed. They grew in my mind. They seemed to have been made by the largest foot a man ever had. The thought held my breath. "Wisht Poppy was here," I said.

The baby sat up, round-eyed, blinking.

Mother spoke, making talk. "I wonder what name your father's going to bring this chap. I promised him the naming."

"He'll fotch a sour 'un," Fern grudged. "Ooge, Boll, Zee. One like smut-face little 'uns wear at the mines."

"I told your father, 'Name him for an upstanding man. A man clever, with heart and pride.'"

"Hope it's a rhymer," I said. "Whoever named them fourteen Crownovers was clever. Hit tuck a head full o' sense to figure all o' them."

"Once I knew a man who had a passel o' children," Mother related. "He married two times and pappyed twenty-three. After there come sixteen, he ran out o' names. Just called them numbers, according to order. Seventeen, eighteen, nineteen, twenty—" She paused, watching baby. He slept, leant upon nothing, like a beast sleeps.

"If Poppy was here," Fern yawned, "I bet he'd laugh."

"You'll all be dozing on foot before long," Mother told us. "Time to pinch the wick."

The lamp was smothered; we crawled between covers. Once the light died the window hole turned gray. You could see the shoulders of hills through it. Fern and Lark hushed and slept. I lay quiet, listening, and my ears were large with dark, catching midges of sound. The shuck mattress ticked, ticked, ticked. A rooster crowed. Night wore.

In my sleep I heard the mare thresh in her stall, pawing the ground with a forefoot. I raised on an elbow. From behind the barn came an owly cough, and a voice saying, "Hold!" Someone stood inside the window, tall, white-gowned. It was Mother. I sprang beside her, looking. Fellows topped the ridge as ants march, up and over. Their heads were like folks' heads, but their backs were humpty.

"Six walkers with pokes," Mother said, "carrying only God knows what."

I recollect waking with the sun in my face; I recollect thinking Father would come home that day, bringing the frames to set against robbers and bloom winters. Lark was asleep beside me, and Fern and the baby lay in Mother's bed with their heads on a duck pillow. I recollect glancing through the window and seeing Mother run out of the fields.

I stood in my shirttail as Mother swung the door. Her hair fell wild about her shoulders. For a moment she had no breath to speak. "The mare's gone!" she gasped. "Gone."

Fern roused, meany for being awakened with a start. Lark's eyes opened, damp and large.

"I propped the stall door," I vowed. "Hit was latched and propped too."

"Had Poppy been at home," Fern quarreled, "stealers wouldn't a-come."

"I'd have figured she broke the latch of her own free will," Mother said, "hadn't it been for where the tracks led. I followed."

"Was they brogan prints alongside?" I asked. They grew immense in my mind. "Bigger'n anything?"

"Just bare mare tracks. I followed within sight o' the Crownovers'."

Of a sudden I scorned the Crownovers. I could hear blood drum my ears. I said, "If I met one o' them chaps, I'd not know him from dirt. I'd not speak a howdy."

Fern twisted into her garments. "I bet them girl-chaps wear old flour-sack dresses, and you kin read print front and back." She wrinkled her nose, making to cry. "I'm wanting to move to Houndshell." She flicked her eyelids, but not a tear would come. She got angry, angry as I. "Ruther be dust in a grave box than have to do with them folks. Be my name theirs, I couldn't hold up my head for shame."

"Don't lay blame for shore," Mother warned. "The mare's tracks went straight, yet they might o' veered a bit this side. There's nothing we can settle till your father's here, and he aimed to stop by Crownovers' anyhow."

Fern stamped her feet against the floor. "I wisht this house would burn to ashes. We'd be bound to live at the mines where they's girls to play with, and hain't no robbers."

"Ramshack house, a-setting on a rock," I mocked.

Mother turned hurt eyes upon us. She stood before the cold fireplace and began to lay off with hands like the Houndshell schoolteacher. "Fifteen years we lived under a rented roof, fifteen years o' eating out o' paper pokes. We were beholden to the mines, robbed o' fresh breathing air, robbed o' green victuals. Now, cellar nor neighbors we've got here, but there's clean air and ground and home. I say this house hain't going to burn. That chimley's to rise higher."

"Poppy ought to be a-coming," Lark sniffled.

"The land not grubbed," Mother lamented, "no seeds planted, the mare stolen. Oh, it's Houndshell for us another winter." She turned away, her shoulders drawn and small.

We children ate breakfast alone, one of us forever peering through the window hole toward the way Father would come. Fern held the baby, giving him tastes of mush. We scraped the pot; we sopped our plates, for Mother had gone into the far room. But she came as we pushed the chairs aside. We stared. She wore Father's breeches. The legs were rolled at the bottom. "I can't climb a ladder or straddle a roof in a dress," she said. "Allus I've wanted to take a hand with this house. Here's my chance, before your father's back. He'd tear up the patch if he knew."

"It's man's work," Fern said grumpily.

Rocks were gathered, clay batter stirred, a ladder leaned against the roof. Up Mother went with a bucket of mud. I climbed, lifting the rocks in a coffee sack, reaching the poke's neck to her on gaining the tiptop. Mother edged along the hip-roof, balancing the sack and bucket. Her face went dead white. Traveling the steep of a roof was not as simple as spoken.

Fern began to whimper, and the baby cried a spasm. "Come down!" Fern called. "Come down!"

Mother buttered two rocks with clay, placing them on the chimney. They rolled off, falling inside. She was slapping mud to a third when a voice roared beside the house. A man stood agape. A stranger had come unbeknownst. Mother jerked, and the bucket slipped, and the coffee sack emptied in a clatter across the shingles. The fellow had to jump limber dodging that rock fall. He roared, laughing, "Come down, woman, afore you break yore neck!" Mother obeyed, red-faced, ashamed of the breeches she wore.

We studied the man. He was older than Father, smaller, and two hands shorter. His eyes were bright as new ten-pennies. An empty pipe stuck out of his mouth, the bowl a tiny piggin carved from an oak boss. "When a woman undertakes man's gin-work," he spoke, "their fingers all turn to thumbs." He didn't stand back. He hauled rocks and a new batch of clay up the ladder; he fashioned that chimney to a fare-you-well.

Lark and Fern and I whispered together.

Fern asked, "Who be this feller?"

Lark ventured, "Hit might be Old Bloody Tom, come for a coal o' fire."

I mouthed words in their ears. "I'd vow he's not a Crownover. His feet hain't big enough."

"We're obliged," Mother said when the stranger descended. She wore a dress now, though she was still abashed.

The man bowed his arms, tipped the pipe, discounting. "A high perch I've needed to search about. A horse o' mine broke stable last night. I'm looking for him."

Lark raised on his toes, straining to tell of our mare. Mother hushed him with a glance.

"Animals are apt to go traipsing with another nigh," the man continued, eying the barn, "but they usually come home by feeding time. Like as not, they'll bring in a furren critter, and it's a puzzle to whom they're belongen. I allus said, men and beast air cut from the same ham." He bent his knees to glance under the house, and grunted knowingly. He shuffled to go. "Yonder atop the roof I beheld you've got a sight o' grubbing to do. Hit'd take Methuselum's begats to ready that ground for seed." He started off, speaking over his shoulder, "If you had fitten neighbors, they'd not fail to help." He went down-hill and up-creek, and we watched him out of sight.

We set a steady lookout for Father. As the hours crept into afternoon Mother complained, her voice at the rag edge of patience, "Your father ought to come while daylight's burning."

But Father arrived when the bull-bats were flying and night darkened the hollows, and he came alone and empty-handed. No windowframes he brought. I recollect he smiled on seeing our glum faces in the light of the great fire Mother had built. Even baby sulled a mite.

"What bush did you get them pouts off of?" he asked.

Mother lifted her hands in defeat. "I'm a-mind we'll have to endure the camps a spell longer."

"Hark!" Father exclaimed. How strangely he looked at Mother, at us all. The mulligrubs were writ deep upon our faces.

"The mare stolen, no chance for a crop. Oh, the sorriest of folks we've moved nigh."

"Hark-o!"

"Them Crownovers hain't fitten neighbors," Fern scoffed. "A man come a-saying it."

I spoke with scorn, "They've got rhymy chaps. Their names sound like an old raincrow hollering '*cu cu cu, cucucu.*'"

"A man come a-saying—"

"Even if the garden and crop were planted," Mother despaired, "there'd be no place earthy to store winter food."

Father grinned. "Why, we've got a cellar dug by the Man Above. Old Izard Crownover says it's yonder in that brushy draw—a cave hole in solid limerock that'll keep stuff till Glory. Now he ought to know."

Our mouths fell open. We could scarcely believe.

"Ah, ho," Father chortled, swinging the baby onto his shoulder. "They's another thing we've got for sartin, and that's a name for this little tadwhacker. He's to be named for a feller proud as ever walked. I'm going to call him Zard, after Old Izard."

"A man come a-saying—"

"Old Izard himself," Father said. "Why, them Crownovers are so proud they dreaded telling us o' using our cave for a cellar. They called hit trespassing. Walked their stuff out in the black o' night."

"The mare might o' broke the latch," Mother admitted, "but her tracks went straight as a measure."

"Come morning," Father chuckled, "you kin look up Shoal Creek, and there'll be the mare and Crownover's stally hauling windowframes in a wagon. And there'll be Old Izard and his woman and all his rhymers a-walking, coming to help grub, plow, and seed. Such an ant bed o' folks you'll swear hit's Coxey's Army."

Father halted, remembering what Izard had told him. He eyed Mother and began to laugh. Laughter boiled inside of him. He could barely make words, so balled his tongue was. "From now on," he gulped, "thar's one thing for shore." He threshed the air, his face fiery with joy. "I'm the one wearing the breeches." He struggled for breath. He choked.

Mother struck the flat of her hands against his back. "The nature of a man is a quare thing," she said.

# Locust Summer

I recollect the June the medicine drummer and his woman came down Shoal Creek and camped three days in our mill. That was the summer of Mother's long puny spell after the girl-baby was born; it was the time seventeen-year locusts cried *"Pharaoh"* upon the hills, and branches of oak and hickory perished where their waxy pins of eggs were laid. Wild fruit dried to seeds, and scarcely would birds peck them, so full their crops were with nymphs. Mulberries in the tree behind our house ripened untouched. Lark and I dared not taste, fearing to swallow a grub. Fern vowed not to eat, though I remember her tongue stayed purple till dog days.

"A rattlesnake's less pizenous than berries in a locust season," Mother kept warning. She knew our hunger; she knew how sorry Father's cooking was. "A body darst eat off o' vine or tree."

"A reg'lar varmint and critter year," Father told Mother. "Aye gonnies, if they hain't nigh as many polecats in the barn as they's locust amongst trees. Yet nothing runs as wild as these chaps. Clothes a puore tear-patch, hands rusty as hinges. Hit'll be a satisfaction when you're able to take them back under your thumb. I'd a'soon tend a nest o' foxes."

"I figure to strengthen when the locusts hush," Mother said. "A few more days o' roaring and they'll be gone." And she glanced at Fern, being most worried about her. "Still, I can't make a child take pride if they're not born with it. Fern's hair is matty as a brush heap. It's eating her eyes out."

"Humph," Fern said. She didn't care a mite.

Lark and I would look scornfully at the baby nestled in

the crook of Mother's arm. We'd poke our lips, blaming it for our having to eat Father's victuals. Oft Zard would crawl under the bed to sniffle, and Mother had to coax him out with morsels from her plate. He was two years old, and jealous of the baby. Fern never complained. She fetched milk and crusts to her hidden playhouse, eating little at the table. So it was Lark and I who stubbed at meals. A pone Father baked was a jander of soda. Vegetables were underdone or burnt. We would quarrel, saying spiteful things of the baby, though above our voices rose the screams of the locusts, *"Phar-rrr-a-oh! Pha-rrr-a-oh!"* The air was sick with their crying.

Father would blink at Mother. He'd hold his jaws, trying to keep a straight face. "No sense raising a babby nobody wants," he'd speak. "Wish I could swap her to a new set o' varmint traps. Or could I find a gypsy, I'd plumb give her away."

"I'd ruther to have a colt than a basketful o' baby chaps," I'd say. "I allus did want me one." I would think of our mare, and the promise Father once made. Long past he'd made it, longer than hope could live. He'd said, "Some fine pretty day thar might be a foal. Hit's on the books." But never would he say just when, never say it was a sure fact.

I recollect that on the morning the medicine drummer and his woman came down Shoal Creek I had gone into the bottom to hunt Fern's playhouse. She had bragged of it, nettling me with her talk. "A witch couldn't unkiver my den," she'd said. "I got something there that'd skin yore eyes."

I was searching the berry thicket when a dingle-dangle sounded afar. A spring wagon rattled the stony creek-bed, pulled by a nag so small I could hardly believe it, and a man and woman rode the jolt seat. It passed the mill, climbing the steep road to our house. I watched it go, and hurried after; I ran, hoping it came unbeknownst to Fern.

But Fern was there before me, staring. Mother came onto the porch, taking her first steps in weeks. She held the baby, squinting in the light, her face pale as candlewax. Zard peeped around her skirts.

The drummer jumped to the ground, his hat crimped in a hand. He was oldy, and round-jawed as a cushaw is round, and not a hair grew on the pan of his head; he was old and his woman seemed young enough to be a daughter. He bowed to Mother, brushing his hat against the dirt. He spoke above the thresh of locusts, eying as if taking a size and measure. "Lady," he said, "could we bide a couple o' nights in your millhouse, we'd be grateful. My pony needs rest." The woman gazed. Her hair hung in plaits. She watched the baby in its bundle of clothes.

Mother sat down on the water bench. She couldn't stay afoot longer. "You're welcome to use," she replied. "A pity hit's full o' webs and meal dust. My man's off plowing, else he'd clean the brash out."

I couldn't hold my eyes off the nag, off the tossy mane that was curried and combed. She looked almost as pretty as a colt.

Fern edged nearer, anxious. "Lizards in that mill have got razor throats. You're liable to get cut at."

"We can pay," the drummer said to Mother.

"Not a pency-piece we'd take," Mother assured.

Fern became angry, and I marveled at her. She doubled fists behind her back. "Spiders beyond count in the mill. Spiders a-carrying nit bags and stingers."

"Lady," the drummer said, speaking to Mother and paying Fern no attention, "I've traveled a far piece in my life." He stacked his hands cakewise. "A host of sicknesses I've seen. Now, when a body needs a tonic, when their nerves stretch, I can tell on sight. I've seen women's flesh fall away like a snow melt. I've seen—"

"Doc Trawler!"

The woman had called from the wagon, calling a bit shrill and quick, tossing her plaits uneasily. She had seen Mother's face grow whiter than puccoon blossoms.

"Ask about the berries."

"Ah, yes," the drummer said irritably, dropping his hands. "My wife's a fool for berry cobbler. She's bound to eat

though one seed can cause side-complaint. My special purge
has saved her being stricken long ago."

"Ask may we pick berries in the bottom!" The woman's
words cracked like broken sticks.

The drummer waited.

Mother stirred uncertainly. "Wild fruit's pizen as stric-
kynine when locusts swarm," she cautioned. "Allus I've
heard that."

The drummer's face lit, grinning. He swept his hat onto
his head and climbed on the wagon. The woman smiled too,
but it was the baby she smiled at.

"That mill's a puore varmint den," Fern spoke hatefully.

The pony wheeled, and they set off for the mill. The
drummer's woman looked back, her eyes hard upon the
baby.

That night we children sat at the table with empty plates.
Grease frizzled the dove Father was cooking for Mother.
"They hain't a finickier set o' chaps in Kentucky," Father
groaned. "I bile stuff by the pot, I bake and I fry, still these
young 'uns will hardly eat a mouthful. By jukes, if I don't
believe they could live on blue air."

I wrinkled my nose. A musky smell came from somewhere. I spied at the bowl of potatoes, at the bud eyes staring.
"I hain't hungry," I said, but I was. Hunger stalked inside of
me.

The musk grew. Lark and Zard pinched their noses and
grunted. Yet Fern didn't seem to mind. She spread her hands
flat upon her plate, and they were pieded with candle-drip
warts.

I grew envious of the warts. I bragged, "I've got a spool
will blow soap bubbles the size o' yore head."

"Baby's got the world beat for bubbles," Father said.
"Blows 'em with her mouth."

"A varmint's nigh," Mother said, covering the baby's
face. She rocked her chair by the stove to fan the smell.
"Traps ought to be set under the house."

Father poked a fork into the dove. "I met a skunk in the

barn-loft," he chuckled. "Stirred the shucks and out she come, tail high. I reckon it's my pea jacket by the door riching the wind."

"Polecats have got the prettiest tails of any critter," Fern defended. "Hain't allus a-miaowing like nannies."

"Their tails are not bonny as the drummer-pony's mane," I said.

"Haste that garment to the woodpile," Mother told me.

I snatched the jacket and went into the yard, leaving it on the chopblock. I looked about. The mulberry tree stood black-ripe with dark. Below, in the bottom, the mill cracks shone. I planned, "Come morning, I'll get a close view o' that nag. I'll say to the drummer, 'Was Poppy of a notion, would you swap to our mare?'" I spat, thinking of our beast.

Father was talking when I got back. "I've set traps the place o'er, but every day they're sprung, bait gone, and nothing snared. I say hit's a question. The only thing I've caught's an old she in the millhouse, and I figure little ones were weaned."

"Once I seed two varmints walking," Lark said. "I run, I did."

Fern stuck her chin out, vengeful and knowing. "I told them folks that mill was a puore den."

Mother saddened. "I've never heard a child talk so brashy to olders. I was ashamed."

Fern raised her hands, tick-tacking fingers. "Humph," she said willfully.

The thought came into my head that Fern's playhouse might be close to the mill. I stung to go and see.

"One thing's gospel," Father laughed, not wanting Mother to begin worrying, "chaps nor varmints won't tetch my bait. I load the traps and table, for nothing. They're independent as hogs on ice."

"These chaps are slipping out o' hand," Mother said, her lips trembling. "Fern, in partic'lar. Eleven years old and not a sign o' womanly pride. I can't recollect the last time she combed her hair."

"Might's well buy her breeches and call her a boy," Father teased, "yet I'm a-mind she'll break over. Girls allus get prissy by the time they're twelve. Hit's on the books." He eyed Lark and me. "I know two titmice hain't combed their topknots lately."

"You ought to make Fern wear plaits," I spoke. "The drummer's woman wears 'em."

"I hain't going to weave myself to ropes," Fern said. She walked fingers around her plate, skippety-hop. "Hair tails hanging. Humph! Ruther to be baldy."

"Ah, ho," Father laughed. "I come by the mill before dark and talked to Doc Trawler. I saw him with his hat off. Now, his woman don't need a looking-glass. She kin just say, 'Drap yore head down, old man. I aim to comb my lockets.'"

"Once I seed a horse go by with a wove tail," Lark said.

The dove browned, and was lifted to a plate. Father handed it to Mother. The bird was small, hard-fried, and briny it was bound to taste. Father always seasoned with a heavy hand. I thought, "It would take a covey o' doves to satisfy me." I felt that empty. I thought of berries wasting in the bottom; I thought of the mulberry tree. I spooned a half-cooked potato from the bowl, speaking under my breath, "That baby's to blame. She hain't nothing but a locust-bug."

Mother fiddled with the bird. Zard slid off the bench to get a morsel. Presently Mother gave it all to him, saying, "I can't stir an appetite. I can't force it down."

Father groaned. "Be-dabs, if the whole gin-works hain't got the punies. Even the mare tuck a spell today. She wouldn't eat corn nor shuck."

"What ails the mare?" Mother asked quietly. The baby had whimpered in her nap.

I didn't pity the beast, being contemptuous of her. I scoffed, "Bet they's folks would say hit's writ in a book. Now, they's no book got everything printed already."

Father answered neither Mother nor me, but his eyes were sharp and bright. He said, "I forgot that drummer sent a bottle o' tonic. Swore it'd red the blood and quick the appetite. Hit's yonder in my pea jacket. One o' you fellers fotch it."

"I be to go," Lark said. He brought in a tall bottle of yellow medicine.

Father held the bottle aloft, jesting, "If this would arouse hunger, I'd dose chaps, traps, and the mare. Allus been said, when the sick take to eating, they're nigh well. A shore promise." He set the bottle on a high shelf and chuckled. "I wonder from what creek Doc Trawler dipped that yaller water."

"Is the mare's sickness natural?" Mother insisted.

"I heard a gander honk last fall," Father said, "but hit's no sign we've got a goose nest."

Lark said, "I bet she up and et berries."

"Old plug mare," I mumbled. I spoke aloud, "That drummer's got a healthy nag. Hain't much bigger'n a colt. Was she mine, I'd not swap for gold."

"I glimpsed that play-pretty of a nag," Father said. "She's old as Methuselum's grandpappy's uncle. Teeth wore to the gum. Thar she was eating out o' a plate, like two-legged folks. If a woman hain't got chaps to spile, she'll pamper a critter to death. The way with women."

The baby waked suddenly, crying. Father leaned over Mother's shoulder. He clucked. "See her ope her eyes?"

I said, "Ruther to hear a bullfrog croaker."

Lark scowled. "Wust I come on a little 'un nested in a stump, I'd run far and not go back."

Fern twickled her warty fingers at me and Lark; she made a hop-frog of her hands. She knew how to rile us.

"Woe, woe," Father moaned. "I reckon we might's well give this child to the drummer-woman and be done. She's got nothing to pet on but that nag and bald-head man."

I looked squarely at Fern. "I've a fair notion where your playhouse is," I said. "I'm going a-searching."

"Humph," Fern said, but she became uneasy. She rubbed her hands together, flaking the tallow warts. "Unkiver my play-nest and I'll get level with you. I'll pay back double."

Mother sighed, "If a pot o' soup could be made tomorrow, I believe I could eat. Soup with a light seasoning." She rocked her chair impatiently as Fern and I kept quarreling. "I long to tame these chaps," she said.

"You'd have to do what Old Daniel Tucker done in his song," Father said. "Comb their heads with a wagon wheel."

The mulberries were ripe. They hung like caterpillars, ready to fall at a touch. I sat high in the tree crotch among zizzing locusts, longing to taste the berries, and watching Fern. I saw Fern crawl under the house; I saw her skitter up the barn-loft ladder. She went here and yon, and was gone, and never could a body tell where.

I hurried toward the mill. The cow tunnels winding through high growth in the bottom were empty. I listened. A beetle-bug snapped and a bird made clinky sounds. I heard digging. A thing went *rutch rutch* in dirt. I tipped-toed; I craned my neck. There amid tall briers the drummer knelt, digging herb roots. The pan of his head was glassy in the sun.

"Did some'un go this way?" I asked.

The drummer rested. Sweat drops beaded his forehead. "While ago a skunk come in smelling distance. I had to stopple my nose." He sorted the roots, pressing them between his thumbs until sap oozed; he frowned and the meat of his jaws tautened. "It's the contrary season to gather herbs, yit a kettle o' tonic's got to be brewed ere I set off tomorry." He plucked a weed sprig from his grab pocket. "Only could I find more o' this ratsbane."

"I know where they's a passel," I said.

His face slackened. "Help me gather some and I'll be obliged. I can pay."

I cut my eyes about, ashamed to say the thing I'd planned. The words pricked my tongue. I took note that blackberries grew large as a toe in the bottom, and both hunger and the pony grew in my mind. "Would you be in a notion swapping your nag to our mare?" I ventured at last. "I allus did want me a little beast."

"Fifteen years we've fed that pony," the drummer said. He arose, stretching his legs. "She's nigh a family member, and my wife thinks more o' that nag than she does her victuals. She'd skulp me, was I to trade."

How bitter I felt toward our mare. "Our critter'll never have a colt like it was promised," I grumbled.

The drummer stacked his hands. He looked wise as a county judge. "She needs a special medicine," he advised. "I mix a tonic that cures any ill, fixes up and straightens out man or beast—the biggest medicine ever wrapped in glass." He patty-caked his palms. "Now, there's one trade I do fancy. Show me where the ratsbane grows and I'll make you a present of a bottle. One's all I've got left."

I spoke, "Bet was a feller to eat wild fruit, a dram o' that tonic would cuore the pizen. I bet."

A woman's voice called from the mill. "Doc Trawler! Oh, Doc!"

The drummer started off. "You stay till I see what my wife's after," he said. I waited, and soon heard him returning, and the cow tunnels were filled with his laughter. He came back shaking with merriment. "That devil of a pony!" he said. "Oh, hit's a good thing we're leaving tomorry."

We went to grabble ratsbane and the drummer chuckled all day. He was a fool about that nag. We dug till my back sprung; we dug till the sun-ball stooped in the sky.

Late in the afternoon we stood by the mill with a poke crammed full of roots. I breathed in the smell of cooking victuals and fairly starved. The drummer slapped the poke; he treated it like a human being. "I'll get your pay," he said, and fetched a bottle out of the mill, a bottle no taller than my uncle-finger. "Hit's strong as Samson," he said. "And wait. My wife's fixing something for your mother."

"Is this medicine bound to work?" I asked, sliding the bottle inside of a pocket.

"Hit'll fix that mare right up, shore as Sunday-come-Monday."

The nag walked around the millhouse. She stuck her head in the door, and drew back crunching an apple. The drummer smiled. "See that thar. Didn't I say this hardtail's nigh one o' the family?"

"My colt's going to have folk sense," I bragged.

"This pony's bound to stick her noggin into places," the drummer said. His face wrinkled happily. The crown of his head shone. "Now, what do you reckon she found this morning? A chap's playhouse. Leave it to a long-nose beast to sniff things out. Me and my wife looked, and what we saw we couldn't believe, but thar it was to prove."

"I'd give a pretty to know," I pleaded. "I've got to larn."

The drummer frowned. "For a good reason I don't want that place disturbed till we leave." He scratched his headtop, undecided whether to tell. "Swear you won't take a look till we're on the road and gone?"

" 'Pon my word and deed."

"Hit's yonder then," he said, pointing to the lower side of the millhouse where the floor rested on high pillars. "I can't blame your sister for trying to scare us with talk o' spiders and lizards. Oh, she's a wild 'un."

The drummer's woman brought a bowl capped with a lid. The plaits of her hair tipped her shoulders, and her eyes were sad as a ewe's. "Reckon we could steal a child off these folks?" she joked her man. "Five in their house. One wouldn't be missed." She handed the bowl to me. "Take this cobbler to your mother. Tell her every berry's been split; tell it's safe to eat."

I ran home, and my heart pounded as I went.

Mother sat alone with the baby. Father stirred soup in the kitchen, and I heard Lark and Zard quarreling there. I uncovered the cobbler, reaching it to Mother. The sweety smell rose in my face. My mouth watered. I spoke loudly, for Mother had plugs of wool in her ears to dim the cry of locusts; I said what the drummer's woman told me to say. The baby leaned to see. Then we heard Father coming, and Lark and Zard following. Mother whispered quickly, "I'm grateful, and hit's a pity to waste, yet we can't trust eating berries. Haste the cobble-pie to the pig pen, and don't name to the others." But time was only left to shove the bowl under the bed.

"All the locusts in Egypt couldn't make a racket equaling these two," Father told Mother. "Fussing o'er nothing but who could blow the largest spool bubble. I mixed hope with that soup you'd soon be up and at these young 'uns. I biled enough to last two days."

"I'll mend once the plague's ended," Mother said. "Any day now the locusts will hush. I long to give these chaps a taste o' soap and water."

"Fern come into the kitchen," Father said, "and it tuck a minute to tell be she varmint or vixen. Hit'd worry the mare's currycomb to thrash the burrs."

Zard peeked at the baby and sulled. He was green jealous. He dropped to his knees and crawled toward the bed. He scampered under.

"Another sight I glimpsed today," Father went on, "and hit was that drummer's woman combing a nag's mane. I never stayed to see if she bowed it with ribbons." He turned upon me, keeping his face sober. "And I've looked up our mare in the books. One more page-leaf to turn before knowing when."

"Only would Fern take a lesson," Mother said uneasily, making a sign. I snatched the bowl, and neither Lark nor Father noticed, for Mother raised the baby's head. Father chuckled, "See the bubble she's pucked with her mouth. Beats any you fellers can blow."

"No bigger'n a pea," Lark discounted.

Father snapped a thumb and forefinger. "Be-jibs, if we hain't got to get rid o' this little 'un. Not a kind word's allowed her."

I stole away to the pig pen, uncovered the bowl, and found the berry cobbler half eaten. Zard had gobbled it. I was fearful, believing him poisoned, thinking he might die. I remembered the bottle of medicine. Could I persuade him to swallow a dose? A thought sprung in my head. I'd dose all— the mare, Mother, and Zard. The drummer had vowed it would straighten out man or beast. They'd take medicine, and not know.

I hastened to the barn, pouring a knuckle's depth of the medicine into a scoop of oats. The mare poked her great yellow tongue into the grain; she ground her teeth. She ate the last bit, and licked the trough. She was mighty fat, I recollect.

On I hied to the house. I tipped inside the kitchen. There was the soup pot boiling on the stove, and I emptied nearly all of the medicine into it. All but one draft went into the soup.

Suddenly a *tick tick* sounded behind the stove. I thrust the bottle pocket-deep, and looked. It was Fern, hidden with a comb in her hand.

"Humph," Fern said, hiding the comb. I could scarcely see her eyes through a brush of hair. She spoke threateningly, "I saw that baldy drummer show you where my playhouse is. If you go there, they's something will scare yore gizzard."

"Humph," I said, mocking.

The next morning the locusts had hushed. Cast skins clung to trunks and boughs, and it was as quiet as the first day of the world. Ere dew dried I waited in the bottom for the drummer folk to go. So great the stillness was, my breath seemed a thunder in my chest. I saw the drummer and his woman climb into their wagon and drive up-hill to our house; I saw Father shake the drummer's hand in farewell. Fern, Lark, and Zard were staring.

I crept to the lower side of the mill where the floor stood high. I crawdabbed under. Nothing I saw in Fern's playhouse, nothing save four stone pillars growing up, and an empty pan sitting. "Humph," I thought.

I heard footsteps. I sprang behind a pillar. Fern came underneath the floor bringing a cup of milk and meat crumbs; she brought the bait from Father's traps. Her hair was combed slick and two plaits tipped her shoulders, woven like the drummer-woman's. My mouth fell open.

The milk was poured into the pan. Fern squatted beside it, calling, "Biddy, biddy, biddy," and four little polecats came walking to lap the milk, and three big varmints began to nibble the meat. I blinked, shivering with fright, and of a sudden the critters knew I was there, and Fern knew. The polecats vanished like weasel smoke.

I recollect Fern's anger. She didn't cry. She sat pale as any blossom, narrowing her eyes at me. But not a mad or meany word she spoke. The thing she said came measured and cold between tight lips.

"You hain't heard the baby's been tuck," she said. "Poppy give it to the drummer."

I stood frozen, more frightened than any varmint scare. When I could move I ran toward the house, running with loss aching inside of me.

I thrust my head in at the door. Father was carving spool pipes for Lark and Zard. Mother ate soup out of a bowl, and her lap and arms were empty. Mother was saying, "Now this is the best soup ever I did eat. Hit's seasoned just right."

Father grinned. "You can allus tell when a body's getting well. They'll eat a feller out o' house and home." He saw me standing breathlessly in the door; he laughed, not trying to keep his face grave. "Well, well," he said, "I've closed the books on that mare. A colt's due tomorrow or the next day. That's a shore fact."

"The baby!" I choked. "She's been tuck!"

"Baby?" Father asked, puzzled. "Why, thar she kicks on the bed, a-blowing bubbles and growing bigger'n the government."

I turned, running away in shame and joy. I ran out to the mulberry tree. The fruit had fallen and the ground was like a great pie. I drew the medicine bottle from my pocket; I swallowed the last dose. I ate a bellyful of mulberries.

# Journey to the Forks

"HIT'S a far piece," Lark said. "I'm afraid we won't make it afore dusty dark." We squatted down in the road and rested on the edge of a clay rut. Lark set his poke on the crust of a nag's track, and I lifted the saddle-bags off my shoulder. The leather was damp underneath.

"We ought ne'er thought to be scholars," Lark said.

The sun-ball had turned over the hill above Riddle Hargin's farm and it was hot in the valley. Grackles walked the top rail of a fence, breathing with open beaks. They halted and looked at us, their legs wide apart and rusty backs arched.

"I knowed you'd get dolesome ere we reached Troublesome Creek," I said. "I knowed it was a-coming."

Lark drew his thin legs together and rested his chin on his knees. "If'n I was growed up to twelve like you," he said, "I'd go along peart. I'd not mind my hand."

"Writing hain't done with your left hand," I said. "It won't be ag'in' you larning."

"I oughtn't to tried busting that dinnymite cap," Lark said. "Hit's a hurting sight to see my left hand with two fingers gone."

"Before long it'll seem plumb natural," I said. "In a little spell they'll never give a thought to it."

The grackles called harshly from the rail fence.

"We'd better eat the apples while we're setting," I said. Lark opened the poke holding a Wilburn and a Henry Back.

"You take the Wilburn," I told him, for it was the largest. "I choose the Henry Back because it pops when I bite it."

Lark wrapped the damp seeds in a bit of paper torn from the poke. I got up, raising the saddle-bag. The grackles flew lazily off the rails, settling into a linn beside the road, their dark wings brushing the leaves like shadows.

"It's nigh on to six miles to the forks," I said.

Lark asked to carry the saddle-bag a ways, so I might rest. I told him, "This load would break your bones down." I let him carry my brogans though. He tied the strings into a bow and hung them about his neck.

We walked on, stepping among hardened clumps of mud and wheel-brightened rocks. Cow bells clanked in a redbud thicket on the hills, and a calf bellowed. A bird hissed in a persimmon tree. I couldn't see it, but Lark glimpsed its flicking tail feathers.

"A cherrybird's nigh tame as a pet crow," Lark said. "Once I found one setting her some eggs and she never flew away. She was that trusting."

Lark was tiring now. He stumped his sore big toe twice, crying a mite.

"You'll have to stop dragging yore feet or put on shoes," I said.

"My feet would get raw as a beef if'n I wore shoes all the way till dark," Lark complained. "My brogans is full o' pinchers. If'n I had me a drap o' water on my toe, hit would feel a sight better."

Farther on we found a spring drip. Lark held his foot under the cool stream. He wanted to scramble up the bank to find where the water seeped from the ground. "Thar might be a spring lizard sticking hits head out o' the mud," he said. I wouldn't give in to it, so we went on, the sun-ball in our faces, and the road curving beyond sight.

"I've heared tell they do quare things at the fork school," Lark said, "yit I've forgot what it was they done."

"They've got a big bell hung square up on some poles," I

said, "and they ring it before they get up o' mornings and when they eat. They got a little sheep bell to ring in the schoolhouse before and betwixt books. Dee Finley tuck a month's schooling there, and he told me a passel. Dee says it's a sight on earth the washing and scrubbing and sweeping they do. Says they might' nigh take the hide off o' floors a-washing them so much."

"I bet hit's the truth," Lark said.

"I've heard Mommy say it's not healthy keeping dust breshed in the air, and a-damping floors every day," I said. "And Dee says they've got a passel o' cows in a barn. They take and wet a broom and scrub every cow before they milk. Dee reckons they'll soon be breshing them cows' teeth."

"I bet hit's the truth," Lark said.

"All that messing around don't hurt them cows none. They get so much milk everybody has a God's plenty."

The sun-ball dropped behind the beech woods on the ridge. It grew cooler. We rested again in a horsemint patch, Lark spitting on his big toe, easing the pain. Lark said, "I ought ne'er thought to be a scholar."

"They never was a puore scholar amongst all our folks," I recalled. "Never a one went all the way through the books and come out yon side. I've got a notion doing it."

"Hit'd take a right smart spell," Lark said.

We were ready to go on when a sound of hoofs came up the valley. They were far off and dull. We waited, resting this bit longer. A bright-faced nag rounded the creek curve, lifting hoofs carefully along the wheel tracks. Cain Griggs was in the saddle, riding with his feet out of the stirrups, for his legs were too long to fit. He halted beside us, looking down where we sat. We stood up, shifting our feet.

"I reckon yore pappy's sending his young 'uns down to the forks school," Cain guessed. "Going down to stay awhile and git a mess o' fool notions."

"Poppy never sent us," I said. "We made our own minds."

Cain lifted his hat and scratched his head. "I never put much store by all them fotched-on teachings, a-larning quare onnatural things, not a grain o' good on the Lord's creation."

"Hain't nothing wrong with larning to cipher and read writing," I said. "None I ever heard tell of."

"I've heared they teach the earth is round," Cain said, "and that goes ag'in' Scripture. The Book says plime-blank hit's got four corners. Whoever seed a ball have a corner?"

Cain patted his nag and scowled. His voice rose. "They's a powerful mess o' fancy foolishness they teach a chap these days, a-pouring in till they got no more jedgment than a granny hatchet, a-grinding their brains away with book reading. I allus said, a little larning's a good thing, sharpening the mind like a sawblade, but too much knocks the edge off o' the p'ints, and darks a feller's reckoning."

Lark's mouth opened. He shook his head, agreeing.

"Hain't everybody knows what to swallow, and what to spit out," Cain warned. "Now, if I was you, young and tenderminded, I'd play hardhead down at the forks, and let nothing but truth git through my skull. Hit takes a heap o' knocking to git a thing proper anyhow, and the harder hit's beat in, the longer hit's liable to stay. I figure the Lord put our brains in a bone box to sort o' keep the devilment strained out."

Cain clucked his nag. She started off, lifting her long chin as the bits tightened in her mouth. Cain called back to us, but his words were lost under the rattle of hoofs.

"I bet what that feller says is the plime-blank gospel," Lark said, looking after the disappearing nag. "I'm scared I can't tell what is truth and what hain't. If'n I was growed up to twelve like you, I'd know. I'm afeared I'll swallow a lie-tale."

"Cain Griggs don't know square to the end o' everything," I said.

We went on. The sun-ball reddened, mellowing the sky. Lark trudged beside me, holding to a strap of the saddle-bag, barely lifting his feet above the ruts. His teeth were set against his lower lip, his eyes downcast.

"I knowed you'd get dolesome," I said.

Martins flew the valley after the sun was gone, fluttering sharp wings, slicing the air. A whip-poor-will called. Shadows thickened in the laurel patches.

We came upon the forks in early evening and looked down upon the school from the ridge. Lights were bright in the windows, though shapes of houses were lost against the hills. We rested, listening. No sound came out of all the strange place where the lights were, unblinking and cold.

I stood up, lifting the saddle-bag once more. Lark arose too, hesitating, dreading the last steps.

"I ought ne'er thought to be a scholar," Lark said. His voice was small and tight, and the words trembled on his tongue. He caught hold of my hand, and I felt the blunt edge of his palm where the fingers were gone. We started down the ridge, picking our way through stony dark.

# On Quicksand Creek

*A*ARON Splicer drove a bunch of yearlings into our yard on a March evening. Heifers bawled and young bullies made raw cries. We hurried out into the cold dark of the porch. Aaron rode up to the doorsteps, and Father called to him, not knowing at first who he was. "Hello?" Father spoke, and when he knew it was Aaron, called heartily, "'Light and shake the weather."

Aaron opened his fleeced collar, rustling new leather. His breath curled a fog. "If this Shoal Creek mud gets any deeper," he called, "it'll be beyond traveling. A horse bogs to the knees." He slid to the ground, limbering his legs.

Father led Aaron's horse into the mare's stall. He brought a brass-trimmed saddle onto the porch. Aaron shook his boots, loosening mud balls, letting them fall on the steps. His tracks smudged the floors. Mother prepared a meal for him, our supper having long been eaten; and Lark and Zard and Fern pried at Aaron with their eyes. I studied his leather clothes: ox-yellow coat, belt wide as a grist mill's, fancy boots. I'd never seen boots matching the ones he wore. Father had a costly pair, a pair worth eighteen dollars, yet they weren't lengthy, or pin-pointed, or hid-stitched like Aaron Splicer's.

Aaron shucked off his coat. A foam of sheep's wool lined the underside. "Thar's not a cent in yearlings," he said. "Hit's jist swapping copper for brass. Beef steers are what puts sugar in the gourd, and nary a one I've found betwixt here and the head of Left Hand Fork."

"Crate Thompson cleaned the steers out o' all the creeks forking Troublesome," Father said. "I've heard a sketch about him being on Quicksand now. I reckon they's a sight o' beef in the neighborhood o' Decoy and Handshoe."

Mother brought a plate of creaseback beans, buttered cushaw, and a sour-sweet nubbin of pickled corn. Fern raked coals upon the hearth for the coffeepot. While Aaron ate, Father had me and Lark brighten Aaron's boots. We scraped the caked mud away, rubbed on tallow, and spat on the leather. We polished them with linsey rags until they shone.

"I never saw boots have such sharpening toes," Father said. "You could nigh pick a splinter out o' yore finger with them." He thrust his own boots forth to show the bluntness of the shoecaps. "But cattlemen allus crave leather with trimmings."

Our cats leapt upon my knees. They watched Aaron, twitching their whiskers, tensing their spines; they held crafty oblong eyes upon him. I thought, "I'm liable to be a cattle-man when I'm grown up, and go traveling far. Yet it'd take a spell to get used to thorny boots. I'd be ashamed to wear 'em."

Aaron finished eating, wiped his chin with the hairy back of a hand, and walked his chair nearer the fire. Father offered him a twist of home-raised tobacco. He bit a chew, stretching the poles of his legs to the hearth, saying, "I'd take a short cut to Quicksand if I didn't have these yearlings on my neck. Maybe I'd get thar before Crate Thompson buys every last steer." He rubbed his chin stubble; he frowned till his face wadded to wrinkles. "Reckon your eldest boy could round them calves to Mayho town for me? A whole day would be saved."

I raised off my chair, hoping. I was nine years old, old enough to go traipsing, to look abroad upon the world.

"Ho, ho," Father chuckled, big to tease, "you wouldn't call that turkey track of a forked road a town. Now, Hazard or Jackson—" he hesitated, seeing Mother's eyes upon him. The posts of his chair sunk level with the floor. "That's a good-sized piece for a boy to walk alone. Thirteen miles, roundy 'bout."

"I'll pay a dollar," Aaron said. "A whole silver dollar. Silas McJunkins's boy will be at my house with the money when they're penned. Silas's boy is driving two cows down from Augland in the morning."

"I saw Mayho on a post-office map once," Father said. "Hit looked to me like a place where three roads butt heads. But if this town soaks hits elbows in Troublesome Creek, hit's bound to be a good 'un."

Mother sent Fern, Zard, and Lark to bed. Before going herself she brought in a washpan and a ball of soap. Father poured hot water from the kettle, and Aaron washed his face and hands, then pulled off his boots and soaked his feet. His feet were blue veined and white, and his heels bore no sign of rust.

"You've got townfolks' feet, all right," Father said. He picked up Aaron's boots, matching them with his own. "They're the difference betwixt a razor and a froe." He grunted in awe. "Man! These boots are bound to make a pinch-knot out o' the frog o' yore foot."

Aaron champed his tobacco cud. "They're right good wearing," he said.

"When I thresh my oats," Father spoke, grinning, "I'm a-liable to buy me a pair."

I set off behind the yearlings with daylight breaking, and before the sun-ball rose I had reached the mouth of Shoal Creek and turned down Troublesome. The yearlings pitted the mud banks with their hoofs, and I sank to the tongues of my brogans. My coffee-sack leggings were splattered; my feet got stone cold. A wintry draft blew, smelling of sap.

The sun-ball rolled up a hill, warming the air, loosening the mud. The yearlings nearly ran my leg bones off. I cut switches keen to whistling; I hollered and hollered, and I stung their behinds. I herded the day long, knowing then how it was to be a cattleman.

Chimney sweeps were funneling the sky when I rounded the yearlings into Aaron Splicer's barn lot. Dark crept into Mayho by three roads, coming to sit among the sixteen homeseats crowding the creek or hanging off the hillsides. I saw Ark, Silas McJunkins's boy, atop a fence post, eating a straw. Though a boy, he was man-tall. His hair shagged over his collar and hid his ears. And he was as muddy as I.

Ark helped pen the calves, and I got a whole look at Mayho town before night blacked everything. A clever place I found it, with Easter flowers blooming on leafless stems in yards, and bare trees growing in rows. One house stood yellow as capping corn, and new-painted. "If I lived in a town," I told Ark, "I'd choose here."

"Mayho's a wart on a hog's nose," Ark said.

"Trees yonder lined up a-purpose. Easter flowers a-blooming the winter."

"I choose woods God planted," Ark said. He raised his arm. "Hit's growing spring. Thar's chimley sweeps raising spit to glue their nests."

We beat on Splicer's kitchen door. Aaron's woman opened it a crack, but we didn't cross the sill, for she saw our muddy clothes and told us to sleep in the barn. She handed us a plate of cold hand-pies, and a rag bag of a quilt. We ate the pies in the barn-loft; we burrowed into the hay, leaving only our heads sticking out.

"A mouse wouldn't raise young 'uns in that trampy quilt," Ark said.

I wondered about my silver dollar. Before going to sleep I asked Ark for it.

Ark swore, "Aaron Splicer never give me a bit o' money. He aims for us to drive steers on Quicksand, and said we're to catch a wagon going that way tomorrow. Claimed he'd pay then, and pay double. Two dollars apiece."

"My poppy'd be scared, me not coming straight home," I complained. "I hain't never been on Quicksand. I oughtn't to go." I felt a grain hurt. "Aaron said he'd send me a dollar. A silver dollar."

"He's not paid me neither," Ark said. "He's got us in a bull hole. I've heared he'd shuck a flea for hits hide and tallow, but he'll bile owl grease ere he pinches a nickel off me."

"I ought to be lighting a rag home," I said.

We came on Aaron Splicer a quarter-mile up Quicksand at Tom Zeek Duffey's place. He was waiting for us, and had already rounded four prime steers into Tom Zeek's lot.

"I hain't located Crate Thompson," Aaron said, "but I've diskivered thar's big beef on this creek, head to the mouth. I'm aiming to get it bought and driv to the railroad siding at Jackson in four days. A four-day round up." And Aaron lifted a foot, pointing at his steers. He kicked the board fence, trying the lot's tightness. "I figure I've put the cat on Crate. These brutes guarantee grease in my skillet." He walked the lot, admiring his cattle.

We looked at Aaron's boots. Tom Zeek and Ark laughed a little. Ark said, "Was he to fall down, he's a-liable to stick one o' them toe p'ints in himself. I'd a'soon wear pitchforks."

"I allow they're tighter than a doorjamb," Tom Zeek chuckled.

"Hain't tighter'n the drawstrings on his money bag," Ark said. "I know that for a fact."

"Dude's his nickname," Tom Zeek told us, "and hit's earnt."

Tom Zeek's woman called us to supper. Not a bite we'd had since the day before, except for a robbing of chestnuts from a squirrel's nest. The table held fourteen kinds of victuals, and Ark and I ate a sight. We drank buttermilk a duck couldn't have paddled, so thick and good it was. We stayed the night, sleeping deep in a feather tick.

The next morning Aaron rousted us before daylight. Tom Zeek Duffey's woman fed us slabs of ham, scrambled guinea eggs, and flour biscuits the size of saucers. We set off, with Aaron ahead. Though willows were reddening and sugar trees swollen with sap, a frozen skim lay on Quicksand Creek and rock ledges were bearded with ice. The sun-ball lifted its great yellow eye, warming and thawing, and by midday a living look had come upon the hills where neither bud nor leaf grew. Icicles plunged from the cliffs. Redbirds whistled for mates.

Aaron bargained and bought the day long. We slept on the puncheon floor of a sawmill near Handshoe that night. For supper and breakfast we ate little fishes out of flat cans Aaron got at a storehouse. We started down-creek again, and where it had taken one day to go up, we spent two gathering the cattle and herding them to Tom Zeek's place. We ran hollering and whooping in the spring air.

We rounded eighteen steers and seven heifers into Tom Zeek Duffey's lot. Tom Zeek told us Crate Thompson had come into Quicksand country and was putting up at John Adair's, a mile over the ridge. "Hit might' nigh cankered his liver when he heard Aaron had beat him to the taw," Tom Zeek said. "Oh, I reckon he started soon enough, but he hain't got a pair o' seven-mile boots like Aaron's." He winked dryly at me and Ark.

Tom Zeek Duffey's lot was packed with steers and heifers, being littler than most folks' lots. Aaron drove extra nails in the board fence; he stretched a barbed wire along the posttops; and he sent for Tom Zeek's son-in-law to come and help him drive the herd into Jackson the next morning. "I wouldn't trust this pen more'n one night," Aaron said. "Hit's too small and rimwrecked."

"Why'n't you take these boys on to Jackson?" Tom Zeek asked. "They'll want to spend the money they've earnt."

I said, "They's something I'm half a-mind to buy." Yet I knew two dollars wouldn't be enough; and I knew I ought to be heading home.

"The Devil, no," Aaron grumbled. "I don't trust fences nor chaps. These boys'd scare worse'n muleycows at the sight o' a train engine. Why, if Ark walked the Jackson streets with that shaggy head, they'd muzzle him for a shep dog."

"I jist like to see boys right-treated," Tom Zeek said.

Ark said, "My hair hain't so long yit you kin step on it with them finicky boots. Anyhow, I reckon hit's pay-time. You promised two dollars apiece."

"I'm a bit short on change," Aaron said, embarrassed for having to speak his stinginess before Tom Zeek. "Cash on the line had to be paid for them cattle."

"I'm a-drawing me a line. Lay them two dollars down."

"I'm broke tee-total," Aaron said. "Won't have money for settling till them steers are sold. Why, boys, I figgered you'd be tickled and satisfied with a small heifer for pay. I'll pick you one—one betwixt the two of you."

"You'd pick a runt. Anyhow, a heifer wouldn't rattle in my pocket."

"Hit's yearlings or nary a thing."

"God-dog!" Ark swore angrily. "I hope yore whole gang dies o' the holler tail."

Tom Zeek said, "I allus like to see boys right-treated."

Ark walked sullenly behind the barn, and I tagged along. We sat among dead jimson weeds. Ark chewed a tobacco leaf and spat black on the dry stalks. "I'm one feller Aaron Splicer hain't going to skin. I'm a hicker-nut hard to crack. Some witties he might fleece, but not Old Silas McJunkins's boy Arkles."

"He put the cat on Crate Thompson," I said. "He'll brag now he's sicked one on us."

Ark brightened, opening his mouth. The tobacco wad lay dark on his tongue. "Now, I'm a-mind to go talk to Crate. I bet he could trap Aaron. Hit's said Crate Thompson's a sharp 'un." He grinned, blowing the wad against the barn wall hard enough to make it stick; he strode into the barn and fetched out a pair of mule shears.

I cut Ark's hair. I cut the hairs bunched on his neck, the thick brush hiding his ears, the nest of growth on top of his head; I clipped and gaped and banged his head over.

"I feel most nigh naked," Ark said when I'd finished. "Wisht I had me a looking-glass to see."

We went to the spring behind Tom Zeek's house. Ark

stared at himself in the water between the butter jars and churns. "Looks to me my fodder's been gethered," he said. He lifted a demijohn of buttermilk and drank it down. I raked a tad of butter from a bowl with my thumb and ate it.

After night fell we climbed the ridge to John Adair's homeplace. John and his woman were gone, late-feeding their stock. Crate Thompson sat before a shovel of fire, driving sprigs into a shoe sole. The shoe was a common old any-body's shoe, and not a cattleman's boot. And Crate was hefty as any of Aaron's steers.

"Draw up a chair and squat," Crate said, speaking with tight lips so as not to swallow the sprigs in his mouth. His eyes were intent on Ark's cropped head. Ark sat down, but I remained standing, awkward and restive.

Ark told Crate our trouble. Crate dropped the shoe, lis-tening with a stub finger sunk into the bag of his chin.

"Where's Dude Aaron got them cattle penned?" Crate asked, his words whistling between the sprigs.

"In Tom Zeek Duffey's lot."

Crate spat the sprigs into his hand. Through his gray eyes a body could almost see ideas working in his head. "Well, now," he said slowly, "I can't think o' nothing but a dumb-bull to cuore Dude Aaron."

"Dumb-bull!" Ark cried in awe.

Crate's great chin quivered merrily. "Strip o' cowhide and a holler log and a rosined string's all it takes. But I'll have no hand in it."

"I'll play my own bull-fiddle," Ark bragged happily. "I know how they're made."

"Hit's ag'in' the law," Crate warned.

"Boodle zack!"

"They's fellers roosting in jailhouses for less."

"I'm not aiming to be skint."

"Ah!" Crate sighed, eying Ark's head. "A rare scalping you've had already."

Ark grinned.

"Ah, well," Crate said, breathing satisfaction, "John

ought to have an old hide strip hereabouts." He shuffled away to find one.

"I'm scared to do it," I told Ark. "I'm scared to tick-tack."

"We'll have Dude Aaron calling on his Maker," Ark promised.

"I ought to be a-going home," I said.

We searched the pitch dark on the ridge above Tom Zeek Duffey's barn. Ark tapped fallen trees with a stick until he found a hollow log, a log empty as an old goods box, and with a narrow crack in its upper side. A winged thing fluttered out, beating the cold air, lifting. It complained overhead, asking, *"Ou? Ou?"*

"Scritch owl," Ark named.

Ark set to work on the dumb-bull. He drove twentypenny nails at the ends of the crack in the log; he cut notch-holes in the tips of the hide string and stretched it taut over the nailheads. He worked by feel, dark being mighty thick under the roof of tree limbs. Ark had me resin the hide string while he fashioned a bow of a hickory sprout and a twine cord. The dumb-bull was finished.

We perched on the log, waiting for the cattle to settle. We could hear them moving restlessly in the packed lot, though all were swallowed in blackness. We only knew the direction of the house and barn by the noise of the steers.

Ark said, "Aaron's dropped his boots ere now, and I bet the toes stuck up in the floor like jackknives."

A bird chirped sleepily near us.

"I'm getting chilly," I said. Anxiety burnt cold inside me, cold as foxfire. "We ought to light a smudge."

"No," Ark said. "They'd spot a blaze. I'm jist waiting till them brutes halt their tromp. Hit's best to catch 'em in a nap."

I made talk, hungry for speech. I asked, "What are them towns o' Jackson and Hazard like?" My teeth chattered.

Ark chewed a pinch of bark. "Folks thar a-wearing Sunday breeches on weeky days," he explained. "Folks living so close together they kin shake hands out o' windows if they're of a mind. Humans a-running up and down like anty mars."

"I aim to see them towns some day," I said. "I aim to. Now, I've lived in Houndshell mine camp, yit it wasn't a town for sartin, just houses pitched in a holler."

"I've traveled a sight," Ark bragged. "I reckon I've been nigh to the earth's end. I been to Whitesburg and Campton and Pikeville. I been to Wheelwright and Hyden. Once I went to Glamorgan, in Old Virginia. Hain't that going some'ere?"

I nodded in the dark, thinking of Mayho, thinking of chimney sweeps riding the sky. I thought, "I've already seen Mayho, and I've been on Quicksand Creek. That's far-away traveling." Then we were quiet a long time. I dozed.

A rooster crowed midnight. Ark jumped to his feet. "Hit's time to witch them steers," he said, awaking me. I trembled with dread and cold. I longed to be at home. Ark dragged the hickory bow lightly across the dumb-bull's string, and the sound jumped me full awake. It was like a wildcat's scream, long and blood-clotting and deafening. But that wasn't a circumstance to when Ark bore down. Then it wasn't one lonesome critter; it was a woodsful, tearing each others' eyeballs out. I reckon that squall hustled three miles.

Ark paused. The timber was alive with varmints. A squirrel tore through the trees squacking. Wings flapped and paws rattled brush heaps. Below, in the lot, the steers bellowed. We could hear them charging the board fence, crazy with fear. They butted their heads in anguish, and the ground rang with the thud of hoofs. Yearlings bawled like lost chaps.

"We're not right-treating Tom Zeek Duffey," I said. "We oughtn't to destroy his fence. Now, his woman fed us good."

"A favor we're doing Tom Zeek," Ark said. "He's needed that old rotten-posted lot cleared. He needs a new 'un." And he sawed the hide string again, cutting it rusty. Goose bumps raised on me. A scream came from that log like something fleeing Torment. We heard the fence give way, the boards trampled, posts broken off. The steers lit out, bellowing and running, up-creek and down, awaking the country.

Lamplight sprang into the windows of Tom Zeek Duffey's house, and a door swung wide and the shape of a man bearing a rifle-gun printed the light. The gun was lifted, steadied, and a spurt of flame leapt thundering. Birdshot rattled winter leaves far below us, spent with distance.

"Aaron Splicer'll shoot a lead mine ere he hits me," Ark said, and he dropped the bow and ran. He melted into the dark.

I ran too, trying to follow; I ran plumb into a tree, and fell stunned upon the ground. My head rang, and sparks leapt before my eyes like lightning bugs. When I got up at last, Ark was out of hearing, and there was no sound anywhere. I crept on my hands and knees for a spell. I walked to the ridgetop, skirting around Tom Zeek Duffey's place, coming down to the creek on the lower side. I crept and walked for hours.

Daylight broke as I reached the creek road. Spring birds were cutting up jack, and the hills were the color of greenback money. And there in the road I found a fat heifer. She made a glad moo and trotted after me. I let her get ahead; I drove her Shoal Creek way. She looked to be sugar in my gourd, and a pair of thorn-toed boots on my feet, just like Aaron's.

# The Stir-Off

"COME Friday for the sorghum making," Jimp Buckheart sent word to me by Father. "Come to the stir-off party, and take a night."

Father chuckled as he told, knowing I had never stayed away from home. Father said, "Hit's time you larnt other folks' ways. Now, Old Gid Buckheart's family lives fat as horse traders. He's got five boys, tough as whang leather, though nary a one's a match to Gid himself; and he's the pappy o' four girls who're picture-pieces." He teased as he whittled a molassy spoon for me. "Mind you're not captured by one o' Gid's daughters. They're all pretty, short or tall, every rung o' the ladder." He teased enough to rag his tongue. I grunted scornfully, but I was tickled to go. I'd heard Jimp had a flying-jinny, and kept a ferret.

Jimp met me before noon at their land boundary. Since last I'd seen him he had grown; and he jerked his knees walking and cocked his head birdwise, imping his father. He was Old Gid Buckheart over again. He didn't stand stranger. "Kin you keep secrets?" he asked. "Hold things and not let out?" I nodded. Jimp said, "My pap's going to die death hearing Plumey's marrying Rant Branders tonight at the stir-off. Pap'll never give up to her picking such a weaky looking feller." His face brightened with pride. "I'm the only one knows. Rant aims to hammer me a pair o' brass knuckles if I play hushmouth, a pair my size. He swore to it."

"Hit's not honest to fight with knucks unless a feller's bigger'n you," I said.

"I'm laying for my brother Bailus," Jimp explained.

"He's older'n me, and allus tricking, and trying to borrow or steal my ferret. I'd give my beastie to git him ducked in the sorghum hole."

"I long to see your ferret," I said. "I'm bound to ride the fly-jinny."

"Bailus wants to sick my ferret into rabbit nests," Jimp complained. "Hit's a ferret's nature to skin alive. Ere I'd let Bailus borrow, I'd crack its neck. Ruther to see it dead."

We walked a spell. Roosters crowed midday. We topped a knob and afar in a hollow stood the Buckhearts' great log house, and beyond under gilly trees was the sorghum gin.

Jimp pointed. "Peep Eye's minding hornets off the juice barrel, and I reckon everybody else's eating. We've made two runs o' sirup already, dipped enough green skims to nigh fill the sorghum hole, and cane's milled for the last."

Hounds raced to meet us. We halted a moment by the beegums. On bowed heads of sunflowers redbirds were cracking seeds. Jimp gazed curiously at me, cocking his chin. "You and me's never fit," he said. "Fellers don't make good buddies till they prove which can out-do."

We waded the hounds to the kitchen, spying through the door. Jimp's father and brothers were eating and his mother and three of his sisters passed serving dishes; and in the company chair sat Squire Letcher, making balls of his bread, and cutting eyes at the girls. Jimp told me their names. The squire I knew already; I knew he was the Law, and a widowman. "Hardhead at the end o' the bench is Bailus," Jimp said. "Plumey's standing behind Pap—the one's got a beauty spot." Plumey was fairest of the three girls, fair as a queeny blossom. Her cheek bore a mole speck, like a spider with tucked legs; and a born mole it was, not one stuck on for pretty's sake. Jimp told me all of the names, then said, "I wonder what that law-square's a-doing here?"

We clumped inside. Old Gid spoke a loud howdy-do, asking after my folks, and Mrs. Buckheart tipped the cowlick on my head. A chair was drawn for me, and victuals brought to heap my plate. Bailus leaned to block Jimp's way to his seat on the bench, so Jimp had to crawl under the table. He stuck his head up, mad-faced, gritting his teeth. "Ho, Big Ears," Bailus said. The older brothers sat with eyes cold upon Squire Letcher. The squire was a magistrate and bound to put a damper on the stir-off party.

Gid pushed back his chair and spiked his elbows, watching the foxy glances of Squire Letcher. "We're old-timey people," he told the squire, his words querulous. "We may live rough, but we're lacking nothing. For them with muscle and backbone, Troublesome Creek country is the land o' plenty." He swept an arm toward gourds of lard, strings of lazy wife beans, and shelves of preserves; he snapped his fingers at cushaws hanging by vine tails. "We raise our own living, and once the house and barns are full we make friends with the earth. We swear not to hit it another lick till spring."

Squire Letcher popped three bread balls into his mouth, swallowed, and was done with his meal. He crossed his knife and fork in a mannerly fashion. "Don't skip the main harvest," he sighed in his fullness. "Nine in this family, and none married yet." He smirked, looking sideways at the girls. "But you can't hide blushy daughters in the head of a hollow for long. Single men will be wearing your doorsteps down."

Gid's voice lifted peevishly. "A beanstalk of a feller has made tracks here already, a shikepoke I've never met, a stranger tee-total."

Plumey's cheeks burnt. The mole on her cheek seemed to inch a grain.

Gid went on, "Why a girl o' mine would choose a man so puny is beyond reckoning. I'd vow he's not got the strength to raise a proper living."

Mrs. Buckheart spoke up, taking Plumey's part. "An old hornbeam's muscles show through the bark, but ne'er a growing oak's. And I say you'll ne'er meet a feller with your head allus turned."

The squire flushed merrily. "Gideon, thar's few longing to

shake your hand. You'd put a man to his knees or break bones. Recollect I've yet to clap your paw? Oh, you're the fistiest old man running free."

The shag of Gid's brows raised, uncovering eyes blue as mill-pond water. "One thing I do recollect," Gid said, "a thing going years past when we were young scrappers." He cocked his head. "I recall we battled like rams once. We wore the ground out, tuggety-pull. But it was a draw."

The squire caught the Buckheart boys' hard gaze. He sobered, shifting uneasily, ready to leave the table. Law papers rustled in his pockets. "Gid," he insisted, rising, "you're of an older set. We never ran together, never wrestled as I remember. I'd swear before a Grand Jury."

"I hain't so old I whistle when I talk," Gid crowed. "Hain't so old but what I'd crack skulls with anybody. Jist any sweet time I kin grab a churn dasher and make butter o' airy one o' my sons." A grin twisted his mouth as he got up. "Now, Square, we shore fit. We did." And Squire Letcher and Gid went off arguing into the midst of the house.

"Who invited that walking courthouse?" Cirius blurted.

"Old jury hawk," U Z said.

"He might have come for a good purpose." Mrs. Buckheart chided. "Eat your victuals."

Before we left the table Gid came back. "I've voted the square into going bird-hunting," he said. "Atter his dinner settles one o' you boys hustle him o'er the hills and bring him back so dogtired he'll start home afore dark."

"I'll go," Bailus volunteered, puffing his jaws, mocking the squire. "I'll wade thorns and walk cliff faces. I'll wear his soles off."

"Travel the starch out o' him," Gid said. "I've a notion he oughten to stay on."

"Who asked that magistrate here anyhow?" John asked, his face sour as whey. "They's more warrants in his pockets than a buzzard's got feathers."

Leander said, "He'll plague the stir-off. Fellers will think he's come a-summonsing. And I've heard a mighty crowd's coming across the ridge tonight."

"We've only invited neighbors and a couple o' fiddlers," Gid spoke fractiously, "but a rambling widower is apt to come unbid any place. Yet I'm more concerned about a tender sprig of a feller who's shore to be here, one I'd ruther see going than coming, ruther to see the span o' his back than his face."

Plumey paled whiter than a hen-and-biddy dish. The boys grunted.

Old Gid began to lay down the law. "Girls!" he said, "you're not to throw necks tonight staring at the boys. Sons! We're going to mark the sorghum hole. We're making puore molasses, and no candy jacks. Keep a watch on the kettle."

"I choose pull-candy to sirup," Jimp said.

I thought in my head, "I bet candy jacks would be good."

U Z groaned, "Pap's bounden to dry up the party."

Old Gid's face softened. He chuckled at me and Jimp gobbling pie. "You tad whackers better save a big little spot for the molassy foam."

"Pappy," Jimp asked, "did you and the square sheep-fight once, a-butting heads?"

Old Gid raised his brows and grinned. He stepped to the door and called Peep Eye to dinner.

"I aim to see your ferret," I reminded Jimp. "I want to ride the fly-jinny."

We crept into the smokehouse where the ferret was kept hidden. "A feller can't take a step withouten Peep Eye's watching," Jimp complained, latching the door. In that darksome place I saw giant pumpkins squatting on hard earth, and fat squashes crooking yellow necks. I saw a bin of Amburgey apples, a mort of victuals in kegs and jars; I set eyes on three barrels of molasses. I said, "Them many sirups will turn strong as bull beef ere they can be et."

Jimp whistled a sketch. A furry head lifted above a sack of capping corn. I jumped in fright, and the varmint started, jerking its head down, burrowing into the sack. The ferret wouldn't come out then for all our begging and poking cobs. I didn't get to see the whole of him.

"He's scared," I said.

"My beastie's got nerve spite o' playing timid," Jimp defended. "He'll tackle critters double his size, jist like fisty people. Cagey ones don't show their nerve till they come to a pinch." And Jimp made a wry face, laughing suddenly. He popped his hands together. "I'd give my ferret to see Pap and the square lock horns."

"I'd ruther to see your father shake hands with Rant Branders," I said, knowing by looks that Squire Letcher was snail-weak. "Rant might be tough as whang leather."

"My pap could make Rant eat straw."

"A man's backbone don't print through his clothes."

We listened a bit, our ears against the door; we stole outside, looking sharp. "Yonder's Bailus coming," Jimp whispered, and began to run. I ran after him, though it wasn't Bailus I'd seen. I had glimpsed a girl-child staring around a corner, and she was a Buckheart, for she bore their presence. She had jerked her head away quicker than any ferret.

We ran till the wind burnt out of us; we stopped to rest in a weed patch where noggin sticks grew tall and brittle. "I saw a girl yon side the smokehouse," I said when I could speak. "I bet she heard a plenty."

"Peep Eye," Jimp said. "You can't say 'gizzard' without-en her hearing."

"Reckon she's larnt about Plumey and Rant?"

"Now, no. Hit's the first time ever I did know a thing afore her." Jimp thought a moment. "Was it Peep Eye growed up and marrying off, I'd be tickled. Me, I hain't ne'er going to marry."

"I'm not aiming to be a widow-man," I said, anxious to go to the flying-jinny. I gathered a dozen noggin sticks, snapping them at the root. Their woody knots were like small fists. Jimp picked a bunch too, saying, "Let's crack each other's skulls and see who hollers first."

I winced, dreading the pain, but I wouldn't be out-done. "You hit first," I said.

"No, you."

"I hain't mad. I can't hit cold."

"I'll rile you," Jimp said. He furrowed his brows and spoke a lie-tale. "Yore pappy steals money off dead men's eyeballs, and yore folks feeds on carr'n crows."

I struck, breaking the weed. Jimp cracked one across my noggin. We broke five sticks apiece, and felt for goose eggs on our heads. Then we went on to the flying-jinny at the pasture gap, and there stood Bailus, waiting.

Bailus's face was grave. You could tell he had come begging. "Big Ears," he began, "you ought to lend a hand gitting rid o' the magistrate, else the stir-off will be a reg'lar funeral."

Jimp poked his lips. "Jist a trick to borrow my ferret. You got no use for him bird-hunting."

"The square wants to hole a rabbit or two."

"Hain't fair to skin varmints alive. I'm not loaning, and that's the God's truth."

I studied the flying-jinny, noting its pattern in my head. I felt bound to have Father make one. A long hickory pole it was, pegged in the middle to a sourwood stump. I straddled the limber end of the pole, hungry to ride.

Bailus's eyes narrowed. "I've heard a bee-swarm o' folks are coming tonight, a drove o' people we've not invited. They's something fotching 'em here. Now, loan yore ferret and I'll tell what." He sniffled, but I saw it was make-like. "Creek water hain't dull as a stir-off with a magistrate keeping tab."

Jimp scoffed. He turned toward me. "I'll give you the first ride."

"Fellers!" Bailus spoke quickly, "both o' you hop on and I'll push."

Though Jimp's face grew long with doubt he straddled the jinny. We latched our legs about the hickory pole. Bailus began to push, slowly at first, digging his toes into the ground. As the pole swung clear he pushed faster, faster,

around and around. We sped. We traveled swifter than a live
jinny. A wind caught in my shirt, jerking the tails. I hunkered
against the log; I held on for bare life. The earth whirled, trees
went walking, and tiptops of the mountains swayed and rail
fences climbed straight into the sky. My hands numbed, and
my chest seemed near to bursting. My fingers loosened, and I
was tossed into the air.

I lay on the ground, stupid with dizziness, and Jimp wove
drunkenly, trying to stand. Bailus was nowhere in sight. Then
I saw three bright faces, three girl-chaps melting together.
My lids went blinkety-blink-blink. When my head cleared I
saw it was Peep Eye, alone. She was the spit image of Plumey,
though she had no mole on her cheek; she was the prettiest
human being ever I did see.

"Air you been dranking john corn?" Peep Eye teased.

"I been ding-donged enough," Jimp blurted. "I'd swap
them knucks I'm promised to even up with Bailus."

"He's hasted to steal your ferret," Peep Eye said. "He'll
have it and gone ere you kin catch him."

Jimp kicked the ground in anger. "I wish that critter was
dead and dust. I do."

Peep Eye stood pretty as a bunty bird. Jimp and I leaned
giddily against the jinny pole. Peep Eye said, "I know something you fellers don't. Plumey's marrying Rant Branders tonight."

"Be-doggies," Jimp swore. "Rant promised I was the only
one to know. Secrets nor varmints nobody can keep."

"One secret I've kept," Peep Eye bragged. "I've larnt why
the square's here. A scanty few knows that."

We pleaded with her to tell, but she wouldn't. She would
only talk of the wedding. "When I grow as tall and fair as
Plumey," she said, "I'm going to pick me a man who can
jounce air one o' my brothers, one strong as Pappy, and able
to take his part."

"By doomsday you won't be fair as Plumey," Jimp said
contrarily.

Peep Eye frowned. Her mouth puckered.

"You're the born image of Plumey," I said, "except for a beauty spot. Now, I choose a mole on a woman's cheek."

"I kin make me one out o' a soot pill," Peep Eye said.

"Be-doggies," Jimp grumbled. "I hain't ever aiming to marry."

I sat on the pole and swung my legs. "I'll not be a bachelor or a widow-man," I spoke.

Peep Eye looked strangely at me. She raised her arms and pushed me backward, and fled. I stood on my head yon side the jinny.

Jimp said, "Girls allus let a feller know when they like him a mite."

Under the sirup kettle fire blazed so lively the darkness was eaten away, and pale glimmers of lanterns swallowed, and far tops of the gilly trees lit. I sat on a heap of milled sorghum stalks, my molassy spoon ready, anxious to taste the foam. Jimp crouched beside me, grinding his teeth in anger. He'd heard his ferret was dead, and he stared auger holes at Bailus and Squire Letcher. Oh, Bailus hadn't got rid of the squire. The squire rested on an empty keg, sighing wearily and clapping a hand to his mouth.

I had Jimp point Rant Branders out. Rant appeared barebones, yet in height he stood taller than the Buckhearts. He was long armed and long legged, and a grain awkward. I said, "I bet he's a cagey one. He's a green grasshopper of a man." And I began counting the people who had come to the stir-off. I named my fingers five times and over. I saw Plumey whispering to a bunch of girls, and Old Gid moseying around wondering at the crowd, and Peep Eye flitting here and yon like a silk butterfly. I kept gazing at Peep Eye.

"My beastie's stone dead," Jimp glummed. "That law-square and Bailus's to blame. Had I a chip o' money I'd hire fellers to trick them into the sorghum hole. Be-dogs, I would."

"Fellers'd be scared of a magistrate," I said. "Anyhow, your ferret wasn't shot a-purpose. Hit was mistook for a rabbit."

"My pap hain't afeared o' the Law. He could scare that square in without tipping him."

I caught Peep Eye watching me, and I wanted to leave the sorghum heap. I saw her face was pouty and cold. I thought inside my head, "Hit's not like what Jimp said. I bet she hates my gizzard," but I said aloud to Jimp, "I'm bound to eat molassy foam when it's first done. Hain't but one thing better, and that's pull-candy."

Jimp harped his troubles. "Rant's broke his swear-word. He promised me knucks to fit, and then made 'um shooting big. They'd fit U Z." He fetched them from a pocket and the finger places were the size of quarter-dollars. "I've struck an idee I don't want that fence rail for a brother-in-law. Oh, my pap could jounce him with one arm tied."

"Rant hain't grown yit," I said. "He might grow thick. Already he's a high tall feller."

We went to stand by the sirup kettle, breathing the mellow steam hungrily, watching the golden foam rise. Leander chunked the fire and U Z ladled green skimmings into the sorghum hole. The hole was waist-deep and marked by a butterweed stalk. U Z joked us, "Dive in, boys, and you kin stand yore breeches in a corner tonight." We stepped warily.

Old Gid came with Mrs. Buckheart to test the sirup, spinning drops off of chips, tasting. Gid said, "Stir till it 'gins making sheep's eyes, and mind not to over-bile." He stared unbelievingly at the crowd. "Only a funeral occasion or a marrying would draw such a swarm, and I've heard o' nobody dying. Yet, for a host o' folks, they're terrible quiet."

"Bury some'un in the sorghum hole," U Z laughed, "and they'll liven up."

"I long to see the Law eat a few skims," Leander said, and Peep Eye was hiding behind him, hearing every word.

U Z said, "I'm for giving the oninvited something to recollect this stir-off by."

"Amen," Leander said.

Mrs. Buckheart spoke nervously. "We ought to o' saved a couple gallons o' juice for candy, to please the chaps. We've got more sirup now than can be sopped till Jedgment."

"Invited or not," Gid said, "I want folks to pleasure themselves. What's become o' the fiddlers?"

Leander shrugged. "Ever hear of a fiddler loving the Law? They high-tailed."

Old Gid cocked his chin and spoke low. "The size o' this crowd is onnatural. Something's drawed folks."

Jimp's mouth opened, but he'd no chance to get a word in edgeways. Gid latched his thumbs on his galluses and spiked his elbows. "I'm not a born fool," he said. "Why, I know the magistrate come to speak a ceremony. Everybody knows. Even Peep Eye's got the fact writ on her face." He glanced defiantly at Mrs. Buckheart. "Woman! That spindling Branders stranger couldn't make a hum-bird a living."

Mrs. Buckheart's neck reddened. "Stranger to nobody but you. You've ne'er tested his grit, to my knowing."

"Why a daughter o' mine would choose a shikepoke to live with is ontelling."

Peep Eye emerged from behind Leander. "Plumey worships the dirt betwixt Rant Branders's toes," she said. She threw her neck like a hen; she flicked a spiteful glance at me.

My hunger fled. I thought, "I'll not eat a bite o' Buckheart foam," and I tossed the molassy spoon into the fire. I turned away and saw Jimp whispering to U Z; I saw Jimp thrust the brass knuckles into U Z's hand.

Old Gid snapped, "Tell that young jake to git his growth."

"Speak to his face," Mrs. Buckheart challenged. "Come, I'll acquaint you."

"Sick him, Pap," Jimp crowed happily.

Gid's brows raised. "Ah," he said. His woman had him cornered. "Ah," he mumbled, "I don't mind shaking Rant Branders's glass hand, but first let me blow a spark o' life into the gethering." And just then Jimp raised on tiptoe, calling,

"Looky yonder. They's two fellers rooster-fighting." Two fellows had their feet on marks, their arms doubled. They smote each other.

"Be-dog," Jimp cried, "wisht I was rooster-fighting with some'un my size." We hustled to see, crawling between folks' legs, getting inside of the circle.

The rooster-fighters halted and the gathering made a roar of joy for Old Gid stepped into the ring, walked past Rant, and leveled a finger at Squire Letcher. Gid's voice rose good-naturedly. "Me and the square have a bone to pick. Allus ago we fit, and nary a one could whoop."

A flat smile withered on the squire's cheeks. He'd not the chance of a rabbit scrapping a ferret.

Gid said, "Let's move nigher the fire for light."

The crowd moved, leading the squire; it pushed and spread until the sorghum hole lay inside the ring. The butter-weed stalk vanished. I saw Old Gid's boys bunching behind the crowd, their faces bright and tricky. U Z had left the kettle, edging close to Bailus; and both Leander and Bailus grinned oddly at me and Jimp.

But Gid didn't tip the squire. The magistrate stepped off the marked line, giving up ere he'd begun. He didn't even box his arms. He walked backward, keeping Gid at arm's length; he sidled and crawdabbed until he had sorghum-holed himself. He came out green as a mossed turkle. And then it was Old Gid's boys began pushing, and fellows shoved and fought to keep clear of the hole. Jimp and I were in the midst of the battle. Gid's boys soused a plenty; they soused folk invited or not, and they ducked one another too. U Z grabbed Bailus, rolling him in headforemost; and Leander caught me, and Bailus snagged Jimp. They dipped us.

I wiped the green skims off my face. I saw old Gid walk up to Rant Branders, saying, "Hit's time we're acquainted," and stuck out his arm. They clapped hands. Gid's jaws clenched as he gripped, his neck corded. Yet Rant didn't give down, didn't bat an eye, or bend a knee. He stood prime up to Old Gid, and wouldn't be conquered.

Old Gid dropped his hand. he cut a glance about, chuckling. "Roust the square if they's to be a wedding," he said. "Night's a-burning."

Jimp and I hid behind the cane pile, being too hang-headed and shy to watch a marrying. Under the gilly trees Jimp said, "Me and you hain't never fit. Fighting makes good buddies." He clenched his fists.

I knew Peep Eye spied upon us. "You hit first," I said, acting cagey, taking my part.

"Say a thing to rile me."

I said, "Yore pappy's a bully man, and I'm glad Rant Branders locked his horns."

We fought. We fought with bare fists, and it was tuggety-pull, and neither of us could out-do. And of a sudden Peep Eye stood between us. Her cheek bore a soot mole, and she was fairer than any finch of a bird, fairer even than Plumey. She raised a hand, striking me across the mouth, and ran. Jimp said, "Jist a love lick." The blow hurt, but I was proud. And then we heard Old Gid's voice ring like a bell, and saw him waving his arms by the forgotten molasses kettle. "Land o' Gravy!" he shouted. "We've made seventeen gallons o' candy jacks."

# The Burning of the Waters

WE moved from Tullock's lumber camp to Tight Hollow on a day in March when the sky was as gray as a war penny and wind whistled the creek roads. Father had got himself appointed caretaker of a tract of timber at the far side of the county, his wages free rent. We were to live in the one-room bunkhouse of an abandoned stave mill.

Father rode in the cab with Cass Tullock, and every jolt made him chuckle. He laughed at Cass's complaint of the chugholes. He teased him for holding us up a day in the belief we might change our minds. Beside them huddled Mother, the baby on her lap, her face dolesome. Holly and Dan and I sat on top of the load and when a gust blew my hat away I only grinned, for Father had promised us squirrel caps. Holly was as set against moving as Mother. She hugged her cob dolls and pouted.

The tract lay beyond Marlett and Rough Break, and beyond Kilgore where the settlements ended—eleven thousand acres as virgin as upon the first day of the world. Father had learned of it while prospecting timber for Cass and resolved to move there. To live without work was his dream. Game would provide meat, sugar trees our sweetening, garden sass and corn thrive in dirt black as a shovel. Herbs and pelts would furnish ready cash.

Father had thrown over his job, bought steel traps and gun shells and provisions, including a hundred-pound sack of pinto beans. He had used the last dime without getting the new shoes he needed. He told us, "Tight Hollow is a mite narrow but that's to our benefit. Cold blasts can't punish in winter, summers the sun won't tarry long enough overhead to sting. We can sit on our hands and rear back on our thumbs."

Once Father made up his mind, arguing was futile. Still Mother had spent her opinion. "Footgear doesn't grow on bushes to my knowledge," she said.

"You tickle me," Father had chuckled. "Why, ginseng roots alone bring thirteen dollars a pound and seneca and golden seal pay well. Mink hides sell for twenty dollars, muskrat up to five. Aye, we can buy shoes by the rack. We'll get along and hardly pop a sweat."

"Whoever heard of a feller opening his hand and a living falling into it?" Mother asked bitterly. "By my reckoning you'll have to strike more licks than you're thinking to."

Mother's lack of faith amused Father. "I'll do a few dabs of work," he granted. "But mostly I'll stay home and grow up with my children. Kilgore post office will be the farthest I'll travel, and I'll go there only to ship herbs and hides, and rake in the money." He poked his arms at the baby, saying, "Me and this little chub will end up the biggest buddies ever was."

The baby strained toward Father, but Dan edged between them. Dan was four.

Mother inquired, "What of a school? Is there one within walking distance?"

Holly puffed her cheeks and grumbled, "I'd bet it's a jillion miles to a neighbor's house."

"Schools are everywhere nowadays," Father said, his face clouding. "Everywhere." He was never much for jawing.

"Bet you could look your eyeballs out," Holly said, "and see nary a soul."

Annoyed, Father explained, "A family lives on Grassy Creek, several miles this side. Close enough, to my notion. Too many tramplers kill a wild place. The earth dies under too many feet."

"Tullock's Camp is no paradise," Mother said, "but we

have friendly neighbors and a school. Here we know the whereabouts of our next meal."

Father wagged his head in irritation. He declared, "I'll locate a school by the July term, fear you not." And passing on he said, "Any morning I can spring out of bed and slay a mess of squirrels. We'll eat squirrel gravy that won't quit. Of the furs we'll pattern caps for these young'uns, leaving the tails for handles."

"Humph," said Holly. "I'll not be caught wearing a varmints skin."

Mother would not be denied. "Surely you asked the Grassy folks the nearest school?"

Father's neck reddened. "I told them we'd moved the first Thursday in March," he spoke sharply. "They acted dumfounded and the man said, "Ah!" and his woman mumbled, "Well! well! The whole of the conversation."

"They don't sound neighborly," Mother said.

"Now, no," agreed Holly.

"Upon my word and honor!" Father chuffed. "They're good people. Just not talky." And on his own behalf, "Let a man mention the opportunity of a lifetime and the women start picking it to pieces. They'd fault heaven."

Mother had sighed, knowing she would have to allow Father to whip himself. She asked, "When you've learned we can't live like foxes will you bow to the truth? Or will you hang on until we starve out?"

Of a sudden Father slapped his leg so hard he startled the baby and made Dan jump. "Women aim to have their way," he blurted. "One fashion or another they'll get it. They'll burn the waters of the creek, if that's what it takes. They'll up-end creation."

Daylight was perishing when we turned into Tight Hollow. The road was barely a trace. The tie rods dragged and Cass groaned; Cass groaned and Father chuckled. The ridges broke the wind, though we could hear it hooting in the lofty woods. Three quarters of a mile along the branch the stave mill and bunkhouse came to view, and, unaccountably, a smoke rose from the bunkhouse chimney. The door hung ajar, and as we drew up we saw fire smoldering on the hearth.

Nobody stirred for a moment. We could not think how this might be. Father called a hey-o and got no reply. Then he and Cass strode to the door. They found the building empty—empty save for a row of kegs and an alder broom. They stood wondering.

Cass said, "By the size of the log butts I judge the fire was built yesterday."

"Appears a passing hunter slept here last night," Father guessed, "and sort of fanned out the gom."

We unloaded the truck in haste, Cass being anxious to start home. Dan and I kept at Father's heels and Holly tended the baby and her dolls, the while peering uneasily over her shoulder. Our belongings seemed few in the lengthy room, and despite lamp and firelight the corners were gloomy.

At leaving, Cass counseled Father, "When you stump playing wild man you might hanker to return to civilization. Good sawsmiths are scarce." And he twitted, "Don't stay till Old Jack Somebody carries you off plumb. He's the gent, my opinion, who lit your fire."

"I pity you working fellers," Father countered. "You'll slave, you'll drudge, you'll wear your finger to nubs for what Providence offers as a bounty."

"You heard me," Cass said, and drove away.

The bunkhouse had no flue to accommodate the stovepipe, and Mother cooked supper on coals raked onto the hearth. The bread baked in a skillet was round as a grindstone. Though we ate little, Father advised, "Save space for a stout breakfast. Come daybreak I'll be gathering in the squirrels."

Dan and Holly and I pushed aside our plates. We gazed at the moss of soot riding the chimney-back, the fire built by we knew not whom. We missed the sighing of the sawmill boilers; we longed for the camp. Mother said nothing and Father fell silent. Presently Father yawned and said, "Let's fly up if I'm to rise early."

Lying big-eyed in the dark I heard Father say to Mother,
"That fire puzzles me tee-totally. Had we come yesterday as I
planned, I'd know the mister to thank."

"You're taking it as seriously as the young'uns," Mother
answered. "I believe to my heart you're scary."

"Not as much as a man I've been told of," Father jested.
"He makes his woman sleep on the outer side of the bed, he's
so fearful."

When I waked the next morning Mother was nursing the
baby by the hearth and Holly was warming her dolls. Dan
waddled in a great pair of boots he had found in a keg. The
wind had quieted, the weather grown bitter. The cracks invited freezing air. Father was expected at any moment and a
skillet of grease simmered in readiness for the squirrels.

We waited the morning through. Toward ten o'clock we
opened the door and looked up-creek and down, seeing by
broad day how prisoned was Tight Hollow. The ridges
crowded close; a body had to tilt head to see the sky. At
eleven, after the sun had finally topped the hills, Mother
made hobby bread and fried rashers of salt meat. Bending
over the hearth, she cast baleful glances at her idle stove.
Father arrived past one and he came empty-handed and grinning sheepishly.

"You're in good season for dinner," Mother said.

Father's jaws flushed. "Game won't stir in such weather,"
he declared. "It'd freeze the clapper in a cowbell." Thawing
his icy hands and feet he said, "Just you wait till spring opens.
I'll get up with the squirrels. I'll pack'em in."

The cold held. The ground was iron and spears of ice the
size of a leg hung from the cliffs. Drafty as a basket the
bunkhouse was, and we turned like flutter-mills before the
fire. We slept under a burden of quilts. And how homesick we
children were for the hum of the saws, the whistle blowing
noon! We yearned for our playfellows. Holly sulked. She sat
by the hearth and attended her dolls. She didn't eat enough to
do a flaxbird.

Father set up his trap line along the branch and then started a search for sugar trees and game. Straightway he had to yield in one particular. There was scarcely a hard maple on the tract. "Sweetening rots teeth anyhow," he told us. "What sugar we need we can buy later." Hunting and trapping kept him gone daylight to dark and he explained, "It takes hustling at the outset. But after things get rolling, Granny Nature will pull the main haul. I'll have my barrel of resting."

When Father caught nothing in his traps two weeks running he made excuse, "You can't fool a mink or a muskrat the first crack. The newness will have to wear off the iron." And for all the hunting, my head went begging a cap. Rabbits alone stirred. Tight Hollow turned out pesky with rabbits. "It's the weather that has the squirrels holed," he said. "It would bluff doorknobs."

"Maybe there's a lack of mast trees too," Mother said. "Critters have sense enough to live where there's food to be got. More than can be said for some people I know."

Holly said, "I bet it's warm at the camp."

"It's blizzardy the hills over," Father chuffed edgily. "I don't recollect the beat."

Mother said, "Not a marvel the hollow is cold as a froe, enjoying sunlight just three hours a day. For all the world like living in a hole."

"At Tullock's Camp," Holly said, "you could see the sun-ball any old time."

"And the houses were weather-boarded," Mother joined in. "And my cookstove didn't sit like a picture."

"Now, yes," chimed Holly.

Father squirmed. "Have a grain of patience," he ordered. And to stop the talk he said, "Fetch the baby to us. I want to start buddying with the little master."

During March Dan and I nearly drove Mother distracted. We made the bunkhouse thunder; we went clumping in the castaway boots. The stave mill beckoned but the air was too keen, and we dared not venture much beyond the threshold.

Often we peered through cracks to see if Old Jack Somebody were about, and at night I tied my big toe to Dan's so should either of us be snatched in sleep the other would wake.

In a month we used more than half of the corn meal and most of the lard. The salt meat shrank. The potatoes left were spared for seed. When the coffee gave out Father posed, "Now, what would Old Dan'l Boone have done in such a pickle?" He bade Mother roast pintos and brew them. But he couldn't help twisting his mouth every swallow. Rabbits and beans we had in plenty and Father assured, "They'll feed us until the garden sass crosses the table." Holly grew thin as a sawhorse. She claimed beans stuck in her throat, professed to despise rabbit. She lived on broth.

The traps stayed empty and Father said, "Fooling a mink is ticklish business. The idea is to rid the suspicion and set a strong temptation." He baited with meat skins, rancid grease, and rabbit ears; he boiled the traps, smoked them, even buried them a while. "I'll pinch toes yet," he vowed, "doubt you not."

"The shape your feet are in," Mother remarked, "the quicker the better."

"We're not entirely beholden to pelts," Father hedged. "Even if I had the bad luck to catch nothing the herbs are ahead of us—ginseng at thirteen dollars a pound."

"I doubt your shoes will hold out to tread grass," said Mother.

Coming in with naught to show was awkward for Father and he teased or complained to cover his embarrassment. One day he saw me wearing a stocking cap Mother had made and he laughed fit to choke. He warned, "Shun wood choppers, little man, or your noggin might be mistaken for a knot on a log." Again, spying Holly stitching a tiny garment, he appealed to Mother, "Upon my deed! Eleven years old and pranking with dolls. I recollect when girls her age were fair on to becoming young women."

"Away from other girls," Mother asked, "how can she occupy herself?"

"Stir about," said Father, "not mope."

Holly said, "I'm scared to go outside. Every night I hear a booger."

"So that's it," Father scoffed.

"The plime-blank truth, now."

Mother abetted Holly, "Something waked me an evening or so ago. A rambling noise, a walking sound."

"My opinion," Father said, "you heard a tree frog or a hooty-owl. Leave it to women to build a haystack of a straw."

Mother saw my mouth gape and Dan's eyes round. Without more ado she changed the subject. She prompted Father, "Why don't you go visit the Grassy Creek people? Let them know we're here, and begin to act neighbors."

"They knew we were coming," Father reminded. And he said, "When I have hides for Kilgore post office I might speak howdy in passing."

"The fashion varmints are shying your traps," Mother said, "That'll be domesday."

Father looked scalded. He eyed the door as if on the verge of stalking out. He said, "Stuff your ears nights, you two, and you'll sleep better."

The cold slackened early in April. It rained a week. The spears of ice along the cliffs plunged to earth and the branch flooded. The waters covered the stave mill, lapped under the bunkhouse floor, filled the hollow wall to wall. They swept away Father's traps. When the skies cleared, the solitary trap he found near the mouth of the hollow he left lying.

"Never you fret," Father promised Mother, "herbs will provide. I've heard speak of families of ginseng diggers roaming the hills, free as the birds. They made a life of it."

"I'd put small dependence in such tales," Mother said.

The woods hurried into leaf. The cowcumber trees broke blossoms the size of plates. Dogwood and service whitened the ridges, and wheedle-dees called in the laurel. And one morning Mother showed Father strange tracks by the door.

Father stood in the tracks and they were larger than his shoes. His shoes had lasted by dint of regular mending. He wagged his head. He could only droll, "It would profit any jasper wearing leather to steer clear of me. I'm apt to compel a trade."

"My judgment," Mother said, "we're wanted begone. They're out to be rid of us. They'll hound us off the tract."

"I'm the appointed caretaker of this scope of land," Father replied testily, "and I'll not leave till I get my ready on."

Wild greens spelled the pintos and rabbit. We ate branch lettuce and ragged breeches and bird's-toe and swamp mustard. And again the beans and rabbit when the plants toughened. By late April the salt meat was down to rind, the meal sack more poke than bread, the lard scanty. Father hewed out a garden patch and then left the seeding and tilling to Mother. He took up ginseng hunting altogether. He came in too weary to pick at us and he rarely saw the baby awake. Dan began to look askance at him. As for his shoes, he was patching the patches.

Dan and I gradually forgot Old Jack. We waded in the branch and played at the stave mill. We pretended to work for Cass Tullock, feeding mock logs to saws, buzzing to match steel eating timber. And we chased cowbirds and rabbits in the garden. Rich as the land was, the seeds sprouted tardily, for the sun warmed the valley floor only at the height of the day. Mother fixed a scarecrow and dressed it in Father's clothes. We would hold the baby high and say, "Yonder's Pap! Pap-o!" The baby would stare as at a stranger.

Father happened upon the first ginseng in May and bore it home proudly. We crowded to see it—even Holly. Three of the roots were forked and wrinkled, with arms and legs and a knot of a head. One had the shape of a spindle. Tired though he was, Father boasted, "The easiest licks a man ever struck. Four digs, four roots."

"Dried they'll weigh like cork," Mother pronounced; and she asked, "Why didn't you hit more taps, making the tramping worth the leather?"

His ears reddening, Father stammered, "The stalks are barely breaking dirt. Hold your horses. You can't push nature."

Mother said, "I believe to my soul your skull is as hard as a ball-peen hammer."

Father glanced about for the baby, thinking to skip an argument. The baby was asleep. He complained, "Is the chub going to slumber its life away?" He eyed Dan leaning against Mother and said, "That kid used to be a daddy's boy, used to keep my knees rubbed sore." And he took a square look at Holly and inquired, "What ails her? I want to know. She's bony as a garfish."

"You're the shikepoke," Mother replied. "You've walked yourself to a blade." And she said, "Did you come home early as at Tullock's Camp you would find the baby wide-eyed."

Holly snatched the ginseng and fondled it. "Gee-o," she breathed in delight.

Father caught the baby awake the day he got up with the squirrels. He arrived in the middle of the afternoon swinging two critters by their tails, and he came grinning in spite of having found no ginseng. He crowed, "We'll allow the beans and bunnies a vacation. We'll feast on squirrel gravy." He jiggled them to make the baby flick its eyes. After skinning the squirrels, he stretched the hides across boards and hung them to cure.

The gravy turned out weak and tasteless. Lacking flour and milk there was no help for it. Yet Father smacked his lips. He offered the baby a spoonful and it shrank away. He ladled Dan a serving and Dan refused it. Tempting Holly he urged, "Try a sop and mind you don't swallow your tongue." Holly wrinkled her nose. "Take nourishment, my lady," he cajoled, "or you'll fair dry up and blow away."

"Humph," Holly scoffed, leaving the table.

Father's patience shortened. "Can't you make the young'un eat?" he demanded of Mother. "She's wasting to a skeleton."

"We'll all lose flesh directly," Mother said.

Holly said, "Was I at Tullock's Camp, I'd eat a bushel."

Father opened his mouth to speak but caught himself. He couldn't outtalk the both. He gritted his teeth and hushed.

When ginseng proved scarce and golden seal and seneca thinly scattered, Father dug five-cent dock and twenty-cent wild ginger. He dug cohosh and crane's bill and bluing weed and snakeroot. He worked like a whitehead. Mornings he left so early he carried a lantern to light his path and he returned after we children had dozed off. Still the bulk of the herbs drying on the hearth hardly seemed to increase from day to day. Again Mother reported strange tracks but Father shrugged. "It's not the footprints that plague me," he said, "it's the puzzle."

The garden failed. The corn dwarfed in the shade, the tomatoes blighted. The potato vines were pale as though grown under thatch. We ate the last of the bread and then we knew beans and rabbit plain. Father hammered together box traps and baited for groundhogs. A covey of whitebacks sprung the stick triggers and we had a supper of them. Dry eating they made, aye-o! The groundhogs were too wise.

Awaking one evening as Father trudged in, I heard Mother say direfully, "We'll have to flee this hollow, no two ways talking. They'll halt at nothing to be rid of us."

"What now?" Father asked wearily.

"Next they'll burn us out," Mother said, displaying a bunch of charred sticks. "Under the house I found these. By a mercy the fire perished before the planks took spark."

"May have been there twenty years," Father discounted. "Who knows how long?"

"Fresh as yesterday," Mother insisted. "Smell them."

"To my thinking," Father ridiculed, "scorched sticks and big tracks are awful weak antics. The prank of some witty, some dumbhead."

"We can't risk guessing," Mother begged. "For the sake of the children—"

"Women can read a message in a chicken feather," Father declared. "They can spin riddles of rocks. For my part, I have to see something I can understand. A knife brandished, say. Or a gun pointing in my direction."

Mother threw up her hands. "You're as stubborn as Old Billy Devil!" she cried.

Father yawned. He was too exhausted to wrangle.

The day came when Father's shoes wore out completely. He hobbled home at dusk and told Mother, "Roust the old boots. My shoes have done all they came here to do."

"They'll swallow your feet," Mother objected. "They'll punish." She was close to tears.

"It's a force-put," Father said. "I'll have to use the pair do they cost me a yard of skin."

Reluctantly Mother brought the boots and Father stuffed the toes with rags and drew them on. They were sizes too large and rattled as he walked. Noticing how gravely we children watched, he pranced to get a rise out of us. Our faces remained solemn.

"I'll suffer these till I can arrange otherwise," he said, "and that I aim to do shortly. I'll fetch the herbs to the Kilgore post office tomorrow."

"They may bring in enough to shod you," Mother said, "if you'll trade with a cheap-John." She dabbed her eyes. "A season's work not worth a good pair of shoes!"

His face reddening, Father began sorting the herbs. But he couldn't find the ginseng. He searched the fireplace, the floor. He looked here and yon. He scattered the heaps. Then he spied Holly's dolls. The forked ginseng roots were clothed in tiny breeches, the spindle-shaped ones tricked in wee skirts. They were dressed like people. "Upon my deed!" he sputtered.

Father paced the bunkhouse, the boots creaking. He glared at Holly and she threw her neck haughtily. He neared Dan and Dan sheltered behind Mother. He reached to gather up the baby and it primped its face to cry. "Upon my word and deed and honor!" he blurted ill-humoredly and grabbed his hat and lantern. "Even the Grassy folks wouldn't plumb cold-shoulder me. I'm of a notion to spend a night with them." He was across the threshold before Mother could speak to halt him.

Father was gone two days and Mother was distraught. She scrubbed the bunkhouse end to end; she mended garments and sewed on buttons; she slew every weed in the puny garden. And there being nothing more to do she gathered up the squirrel skins and patterned caps.

The afternoon of the second day she told us, "I'm going down-creek a spell. Keep the baby company and don't set foot outside." Taking Father's gun she latched the door behind her.

We watched through cracks and saw her enter the garden and strip the scarecrow; we saw her march toward the mouth of the creek, gun in hand, garments balled under an arm. She returned presently, silent and empty-handed, and she sat idle until she saw Father coming.

Father arrived wearing new shoes and chuckling. I ran to meet him, the tail of my fur cap flying, and he had to chortle a while before he could go another step. He chirruped, "Stay out of trees, mister boy, or you may be shot for a squirrel." But it wasn't my cap that had set him laughing. Upon seeing Mother he drew his jaws straight. He wore a dry countenance though his eyes were bright.

Mother gazed at Father's shoes. "What word of the Grassy people?" she asked coolly.

"They're in health," Father replied, hard put to master his lips. He had to keep talking to manage it. "And from them I got answers to a couple of long-hanging questions. I learned the nearest schoolhouse; I know who kindled our fireplace."

Dan, hiding behind Mother, thrust his head into sight. Holly let her dolls rest, listening.

"Kilgore has the closest school," Father said. "A mite

farther than I'd counted on. As for the fire, why, the Grassy
fellow made it to welcome us the day he expected us to move
here. But he's not the Mischief who planted tracks and
pitched burned sticks under the house. Nor the one who
waylaid me at the mouth of the hollow while ago."

Mother cast down her eyes.

Father went on, struggling against merriment. "A good
thing I made a deal with Cass Tullock to haul our plunder
back to the camp. Aye, a piece of luck he advanced money for
shoes and I had proper footgear to run in when I blundered
into the ambush." He began to chuckle.

Mother lowered her head.

Swallowing, trying to contain his joy, Father said, "Coming into the hollow I spied a gun barrel pointing across a log
at me—a gun plime-blank like my own. Behind was a bush of
a somebody rigged in my old coat and plug hat. Gee-o, I
traveled!" His tongue balled, cutting short his revelations.
His face tore up.

Mother raised her chin. Her eyes were damp, yet she was
smiling. "If you'd stop carrying on," she said, "you could tell
us how soon to expect Cass."

A gale of laughter broke in Father's throat. He threshed
the air. He fought for breath. "I can't," he gasped. "You've
tickled me."

# School Butter

"IF Surrey Creek ever reared a witty," Pap used to tell me, "your Uncle Jolly Middleton is the scamp. Always pranking and teasing. Forever going the roads on a fool horse, hunting mischief. Nearly thirty years old and he has yet to shake hands properly with an ax haft or a plow handle. Why, he'll pull a trick did it cost him his ears, and nobody on earth can stop him laughing."

But Uncle Jolly didn't need to work. He could pick money out of the air. He could fetch down anything he wanted by just reaching. And he would whoop and holler. Folk claimed he could rook the horns off of Old Scratch, and go free. Yet he didn't get by the day he plagued the Surrey Creek School, and for once he couldn't laugh. He bears a scar the length of his nose to mark the occasion. Duncil Burke taught at Surrey the year Uncle Jolly hallooed "school butter" at the scholars. A fellow might as lief hang red on a bull's horns as yell that taunt passing a schoolhouse in those days. An old-time prank. If caught they were bound to fare rough.

I attended the whole five-month session, and I was a top scholar. I could spell down all in my grade except Mittie Hyden. And I could read and calculate quicker than anybody save Mittie. But she kept her face turned from me. Mostly I saw the rear of her head, the biscuit of her hair.

The free textbooks I learned by heart, quarreling at the torn and missing pages. My reader left William Tell's son standing with an apple on his head; Rip Van Winkle never woke. I prodded Duncil, "My opinion, if you'll let the superintendent know he'll furnish new texts. Pap says Fight Creek and Slick Branch teachers brought in a load for their schools."

A sixth-grader said, "Ours have done all they come here to do."

"Surrey allus was the tail," Mittie said. She didn't fear to speak her mind. "Had my way, I'd drop these rags into the deepest hole ever was."

Ard Finch, my bench mate, snorted. He could hoot and get by, for he was so runty he had to sit on a chalk box. He could climb the gilly trees beyond the play yard and not be shouted down. He could have mounted to the top of the knob and Duncil not said button. And he was water-boy and could go outside at will. Ard wouldn't have cared if books wore down to a single page.

"New texts will be furnished in due season," Duncil said. He believed in using a thing to the last smidgin. He set us to work. I was put studying a dictionary, and I boasted to Ard Finch, "I'll master every word there be. I'll conquer some jaw breakers." But I got stuck in the *a*'s. I slacked off and read "Blue Beard." Short as it was I had to borrow four readers to splice it together.

The next visit Uncle Jolly made to our house I told of Surrey's textbooks. I said, "Duncil's too big a scrimper to swap them in. A misery to study, hopping and a-jumping." And I spoke of another grievance. "Reader-book yarns are too bob-tailed anyhow to suit my notion. Wish I had a story a thousand miles long."

Uncle Jolly cocked his head in puzzlement. He couldn't understand a boy reading without being driven. He peered at me, trying to figure if I owned my share of brains. He tapped my head, and listened. He said he couldn't hear any.

Uncle Jolly rode past Surrey School on an August afternoon when heat-boogers danced the dry creek-bed and willows hung limp with thirst. I sat carving my name on a bench with a knife borrowed from Ard Finch. I knicked and gouged, keeping an eye sharp on Duncil, listening to the primer class blab: "See the fat fox? Can the fox see the dog? Run, fox, run." A third-grader poked his head out of the window, drew in and reported, "Yonder comes Jolly Middleton." There came Uncle Jolly riding barebones, his mare wearing a bonnet over her ears and a shawl about her neck.

"Hit's the De'il," a little one breathed, and the primer children huddled together.

A cry of glee rose at sight of a horse dressed like people and scholars would have rushed to the windows had Duncil not swept the air with a pointer. Only Mittie Hyden kept calm. She looked on coldly, her chin thrown.

I crowed to Ard, "I'd bet buckeyes he's going to my house."

Ard's small eyes dulled. He was envious. Being dwarfish he yearned to stand high. He said, "My opinion, he's going to Bryson's mill to have bread ground."

"Now, no," said I. "He's not packing corn."

"Did I have my bow and spike," Ard breathed, "they'd make the finest bull's-eye ever was."

Uncle Jolly circled the schoolhouse. He made the beast rattle her hoofs and prance. He had her trained pretty. Then he halted and got to his feet. He stood on her back and stretched an arm into the air; he reached and pulled down a book. Opening it he made to read though he didn't know the letter his mare's track made.

Mittie Hyden sniffed, "The first'un he ever cracked."

Duncil tried to teach despite the pranking in the yard. He whistled the pointer, threatening to tap noggins should we leave our seats. He started the primer class again: "See the fat fox? Can the fox see the dog?" But they couldn't hold their eyes on the page. Scholars chuckled and edged toward the windows. And Ard smiled grudgingly. He would have given the ball of the world to be Uncle Jolly putting on a show. He grabbed the water-bucket and ran to the well.

Mittie said, "We're being made a laughingstock."

We quieted a grain, thinking what Fight Creek and Slick Branch children might say.

Uncle Jolly put the book into his shirt and spun the horse on her heels. He pinched her withers and she cranked her neck and flared her lips and nickered. He laughed. he out-laughed his critter. Then he dug heels against her sides and fled up-creek.

"Surrey will be called dog for this," Mittie warned. She wasn't afraid to speak her mind. "It's become the worst school in Baldridge County. Textbooks worn to a frazzle, teacher won't ask for new. Not strange we've drawed a witty."

Duncil's face reddened. He was stumped.

"Uncle Jolly is smart as ants," I defended, "and his mare is clever as people."

Mittie darted a glance at me. She closed her teeth and would say no more.

Hands raised the room over, begging leave to talk. Scholars spoke unbidden:

"I seed a bench-legged dog once, trained to raise and walk on her hind legs. Upon my word and honor, she had a peck o' brains."

"One day my mom passed Jolly Middleton and he was all hey-o and how-are-ye. He tipped his hat, and out flew a bird."

"Biggest fun box ever was," my pap claims.

Rue Thomas began, "Once on a time there was a deputy sheriff aimed to arrest Jolly Middleton—"

Duncil found his tongue. "I grant there's a nag with more gumption than her master. Now, hush."

Ard fetched in a bucket of water. He whispered to me, "Tomorry I'm bringing my bow and spike for shore."

Rue Thomas tried again, "Once the Law undertook to corner Jolly Middleton—"

"Hush!" Duncil ordered. He lifted his chin, rummaging his mind for a way to sober us. He noted the hour—thirty minutes until breaking. He said presently, "We'll have a sea-

son of story-telling to finish the day. Accounts of honor and
valor." He nodded at Mittie. "Young lady, take the floor and
lead with the history of the Trojan horse in days of yore."

Mittie stood and went forward without urging. I hark-
ened although I opened the dictionary and pretended to
study. She told of the Greeks building a mighty wooden nag,
hollow as a gourd, and with a door in its belly; of the critter
getting drawn into Troy-town for a sight to see, and warriors
climbing forth at night and sticking spears through everybody. We listened, still as moss eating rocks.

When school let out I ran the whole way home. Pap sat on
the porch and the rocker of his chair was scotched by a book.
Before I could quit chuffing he announced, "That scamp of
an uncle has been here again. And he has confounded creation by doing a worthy deed. He's talked the superintendent
into promising new texts for Surrey, and you're to notify
Duncil Burke."

I stared at the book, too winded to speak.

Pap bent to free the rocker. Raising the volume he added,
"And Jolly says for you to read this till your head rattles."

I seized the book. A giant strode the cover, drawing ships
by ropes and the title read, "Gulliver's Voyage to Lilliput." I
opened the lid, eyes hasting: "My father had a small estate in
Nottinghamshire; I was the third of five sons. . . ."

I wore it like a garment. Under my pillow it rested at
night, clutched in my hand it traveled to school of a day. I
turned stingy. I wouldn't loan it, declaring, "I'll be the only
feller fixed to tell about Lemuel Gulliver and what he done.
I'm bound it will cap any old wooden horse yarn."

Ard said, "Rather to see a person cutting up jake on a
horse than hear a lie-tale. I'd give a peck o' books would Jolly
Middleton come along right now. My bow and spike's waiting under the floor."

I said, "Uncle Jolly could brush off arrow-spikes, the
same as Gulliver did."

"Aye gonnies," Ard swore, "I'd make a dint."

But nine days passed before Uncle Jolly returned, and before I had a chance to relate Gulliver's voyage. By then our textbooks were shedding leaves to match frostbitten maples. Come the slightest draft pages flew. Scholars bundled their books and tied them with string, or weighted them with pencil boxes and rulers. Pless Fowley's child stored her primer in a poke.

When I reported Uncle Jolly's message to Duncil he twitted, "Any news that rogue puts out has a sticker in it. Not an earnest bone in his body, to my judgment."

Mittie tossed her head, agreeing. Yet she mumbled, "I wish a whirly-wind would blow our books to nowhere. Then somebody would be bound to do something."

"The ones on hand will endure a spell longer," Duncil said flatly.

A fourth-grader blurted, "A trustee took notice of my ragtag speller and asked, 'What kind of a pauper place are we supporting at Surrey?'"

"Fight Creek and Slick Branch are making light of us," another said.

"They're calling Surrey a rat's nest."

"Naming us the hind tit."

Duncil's ire raised. He lifted his pointer. "Bridle your tongues," he said, "else you'll taste hickory."

A fifth-grader asked unheeding, "If Jolly comes, what are we aiming to do?" And Rue Thomas opened his mouth to tell of a happening but didn't get two words spoken before Duncil's pointer whistled and struck a bench and broke.

Still when Uncle Jolly passed on a Tuesday morning with corn for Bryson's mill, Duncil gave over teaching. Uncle Jolly rode feet high and legs crossed, and he came singing, "Meet Little Susie on the Mountain Green." A sack petticoat draped the mare's hindquarters, a bow of ribbon graced her headstall, and her face was powdered white.

Pless Fowley's child moaned, "Hit's the De'il, hit is." She

gathered her primer into a poke. Scholars watched, mouths sagged in wonder. Ard breathed to me, "I'm seeing my pure pick of a bull's-eye."

Uncle Jolly rode into the school yard and bowed, and the mare bent a knee and dipped her head. He set her side-stepping, hoof over hoof, shaking her hips, flapping the skirt. She ended in a spin, whirling like a flying-jenny. Then, pinching her withers, he cried, "Fool stutter!" The mare nickered, and Uncle Jolly laughed. He laughed fit to fall. And away they scampered, and while still in view the critter lost her petticoat.

A scholar sang out, "He yelled school butter!"

"School butter wasn't named," I said.

"The next thing to it."

The upper grades boys leaped to their feet, angry and clamorous, thinking their ears might have deceived them. They would have taken after Uncle Jolly had not Duncil raised a new pointer—a hickory limb as long as a spear.

Duncil brandished the pointer and the scholars quieted. They settled, knowing Uncle Jolly would return directly Bryson had ground his corn. Duncil closed the grammar he held. Until Uncle Jolly went his way it was useless to try to teach. Forthwith he inquired, "Which of you is prepared to entertain us with a narrative of ancient days? A tale to discipline our minds."

Rue Thomas said, "I can speak of a deputy aiming to capture a mischief-maker and what happened. Aye, hit's a good'un."

"It's not what I requested," Duncil said sharply.

Ard's hand popped up. "Here's a feller ready with a tale about Old Gulliver. A back-yonder story." He wagged his thumb toward me.

"Come forward," Duncil invited.

I played shy. I let him beg twice, not to seem too eager. Then I strode to the front. I told of Gulliver riding the waters, of the ship wrecking, and of his swimming ashore. "He took a nap on dry land and tiny folks no bigger than a finger came and drove pegs and tied him flat with threads. They fastened him to the ground limb and hair. And a dwarf mounted Gulliver's leg bearing a sword, and he was a soldier, and brave . . ."

I related the voyage to Lilliput beginning to end, though scholars barely attended my words and kept staring along the road. Whether Mittie listened I couldn't discover, for she loosened the biscuit on her head and let her hair fall over her face.

"Be-dog," a voice grumbled as I finished, "I'd ruther hear the truth."

"Ought to hear of Jolly Middleton nearly getting jailhoused," Rue Thomas said. "A gospel fact."

Duncil groaned. And he checked the clock. There was still time to reckon with. He gave in. "Maybe we can have done with the subject by talking it to death, wearing it out plumb. Say on."

Rue Thomas babbled, "Once Jolly Middleton took a trip to town. Rode by the courthouse and blocking his path was a deputy sheriff ready to arrest him for some antic. There stood the Law, a warrant in his fist. You think Jolly would turn and flee? Now, no. Not that jasper. Up he trotted into the Law's teeth, and he jabbed his beast in the hip, and low she bent to the balls of her knees. He reached and shook the deputy's hand, and was away and gone ere the Law could bat an eye."

A primer child whimpered, "What air we aiming to do when the De'il comes?"

We heard a clop-clop of hoofs and saw Uncle Jolly approaching. He lay stretched the length of his critter's back, a poke of meal for a pillow, lolling in ease. His feet were bare and his shoes dangled at the end of the mare's tail.

Bull yearlings couldn't have held us. We rushed to the windows. Even Mittie craned her neck to see, her mouth primped with scorn. And Ard snatched the water-bucket and ran outside. I thought to myself, "Ard Finch couldn't hit a barn door with an arrow-spike."

The mare drew up in the school yard and Uncle Jolly lay prone a moment. Then he stretched his arms and legs and made to rise. He yawned near wide enough to split. And, in the middle of a yawn, he gulped unaccountably, his eyes bulged, his tongue hung out. He seemed stricken. He began to twist and toss. He yelled, "Oh," and, "Ouch!" and, "Mercy me!" As in torment he slapped his breeches, his chest, his skull.

The scholars watched, not knowing whether to pity or jeer.

Uncle Jolly reached inside his shirt and drew out four crawdabbers. He pulled a frog from one pocket, a granny-hatchet from the opposite. His breeches legs yielded a terrapin each, his hat a ball of June-bugs. He rid himself of them and breathed a sigh of relief. Then he straddled his mare, spoke "Giddy-yap," and started away.

"Humph," came a grumble, "I thought he was going to do a really something."

Uncle Jolly gained the road and halted. He looked over his shoulder and a wry grin caught his mouth and he shouted,

> *School butter, chicken flutter,*
> *Rotten eggs for Duncil's supper.*

Boys hopped through the windows before Duncil could reach for the pointer. Girls and primer children struck for the doors. And Ard came around a corner with a spike fitted to his bow, and let fly. The spike grazed the mare's hip and she sank to her knees, and caught unawares Uncle Jolly tumbled to the ground headforemost. The poke burst, the meal spilled. Up they sprang as scholars sped toward, them. The mare took flight across the bottom behind the schoolhouse, Uncle Jolly at her heels. They ran to equal Sooners. Duncil Burke was left waving a pointer in the yard.

I kept pace with the swiftest. I went along for the running, satisfied we could never overhaul Uncle Jolly, and I traveled empty-handed, having forgotten my book. Uncle Jolly and his beast outdid us, the way we shook the short-legged scholars. They took three strides to our one. And on nearing the creek they parted company, the mare veering along the bank, Uncle Jolly plunging into the willows. When last we saw him he was headed toward the knob.

At the creek we searched the dry bed for tracks. We combed the willows and the canes beyond. We threshed the thicket between the creek and the foot of the knob. And up the knob we went, fanning out, Rue Thomas warning, "Keep your eyes skinned, you fellers. What that mischief will do is untelling."

We climbed to the first bench of the knob and paused to catch our breaths. We looked abroad. We stared upon the schoolhouse roof; we could almost spy down the chimney. From somewhere Duncil's voice lifted, calling, calling. Of a sudden we saw scholars hurrying back across the bottom, crying shrilly. We saw Uncle Jolly run out of the schoolhouse and papers fluttered from his arms like butterflies.

We plunged downhill. We fell off of the knob, mighty near, and tore through the canes. We scurried to join the scholars gathering beyond the play yard. And there under a gilly tree Uncle Jolly lay snoring, a hat covering his face, bare feet shining. The mare was nowhere in sight. Ard Finch stood close, but only Mittie Hyden wasn't the least afraid. She walked a ring around him, scoffing, "He's not asleep. Hit's pure put-on."

The bunch crept closer.

A little one asked, "What air we aiming to do?"

"We'd duck him in the creek if it wasn't dry," Rue Thomas said.

"It would take a block and tackle to lift him," a scholar said.

"He's too heavy to rail-ride," another made excuse.

Mittie accused, "I'm of a mind you fellers are scared."

"I hain't afraid," Ard said, and he moved alongside Uncle Jolly to prove it.

"Better not tip Old Scratch," Pless Fowley's child wailed, and she ran away to the schoolhouse.

Ard said, "I know a thing we can do. Fix him the same as the Lilliputians done Old Gulliver. Snare him plug-line."

"Who'll tie the first string?" Rue Thomas posed.

"I will," said Ard. "Fetch me some sticks for pegs and I'll show you who's game." And after they were brought he pounded them into the ground beside Uncle Jolly's feet. He cut his bowstring into lengths and staked the toes.

Uncle Jolly snored on.

The scholars grew brave. They dug twine and thread out of pockets. They unwound three stocking balls. They fenced Uncle Jolly with pegs and made fast his legs, arms, neck and fingers. Fishing lines crisscrossed his body, pack threads tethered locks of his hair. Even the buttons of his shirt suffered tying. They yoked him like a fly in a web, and still he kept snoring.

And when they had him bound Ard played soldier. He stepped onto Uncle Jolly's thigh and mounted proudly to his chest; he balanced his feet and drew forth his knife and brandished it for a sword.

The hat slid from Uncle Jolly's face. His eyelids cracked. His eyes flew wide at sight of the blade. And of a sudden he bucked. Strings parted and sticks went flying, and Ard teetered. He bucked again and Ard upset and fell, and the blade raked Uncle Jolly's nose from saddle to tip.

We stared, not moving though we heard the mare's hoofs rattling, though we saw Duncil coming pointer in hand. Pless Fowley's child ran among us, holding an empty poke, crying, "All the books have been dropped into the well. Nary a scrap is left." And Mittie Hyden looked squarely at me. She said, "Jolly Middleton is the best devil ever was."

Uncle Jolly sat up. He pinched his nose together, and his face wrinkled with joy. "I can't laugh," he said. "Upon my honor, I can't."

# The Moving

WE stood by the loaded wagon while Father nailed the windows down and spat into the keyholes to make the locks turn. We waited, restless as the harnessed mare, anxious to hasten beyond staring eyes. Hardstay mine was closed for all time and idle men had gathered to watch us leave. They hung over the fence; they crowded where last year's dogtick stalks clutched their brown leaf-hands into fists.

I saw the boys glance at our windowpanes, their pockets bulging with rocks. I spied into their faces and homesickness grew large inside of me. I hungered for a word, a nod of farewell. But only a witty was sad at my going, only a child of a man who valued strings and tobacco tags, a chap in a man's clothes who was bound forever to speak things backwards. Hig Sommers stood beg-eyed, and fellows were picking at him. One knelt and jerked loose the eel-strings of his brogans.

Though women watched from their porches only a widow-woman came to say a good-by to Mother. Sula Basham came walking, tall as a butterweed, and with a yellow locket swinging her neck like a clockweight.

Loss Tramble spoke, grinning, "If I had a woman that tall, I'd string her with gourds and use her for a martin pole. I would, now." A dry chuckle rattled in the crowd. Loss stepped back, knowing the muscle frogs of her arms were the size of any man's.

Sula towered over Mother. The locket dropped like a plumb. Mother was barely five feet tall and she had to look upward as into the sky; and her eyes set on the locket, for never had she owned a grain of gold, never a locket, or a ring, or bighead pin. Sula spoke loudly to Mother, glancing at the men with scorn: "You ought to be proud that your man's not satisfied to rot in Hardstay camp, a-setting on his chinebone. Before long all's got to move, all's got to roust or starve. This mine hain't opening ag'in. Hit's too nigh dug out."

The men stirred uneasily. Sill Lovelock lifted his arms, spreading them like a preacher's. "These folks air moving to nowheres," he said. "Thar's no camps along the Kentucky River a-taking on hands; they's no work anywheres. Hit's mortal sin to make gypsies of a family. I say as long's a body has got a rooftree, let him roost under it."

Men grunted, doddering their heads, and the boys lifted their rock-heavy pockets and sidled toward the wagon. Cece Goodloe snatched Hig Sommers's hat as he passed, clapping it onto his own head. The hat rested upon his ears. The boys placed their hands on the wagon wheels; they fingered the mare's harness; they raised the lid of the tool box to see what was in it. Cece crawled under the wagon, back hound to front hound, shaking the swingletree. I watched out of the tail of my eye, thinking a rusty might be pulled.

Father came into the yard with the key, and now the house was shut against our turning back. I looked at the empty hull of our dwelling; I looked at the lost town, yearning to stay in this place where I was born, among the people I knew. Father lifted the key on a finger. "If a body here would drap this key by the commissary," he said, "I'd be obliged."

Hig Sommers lumbered toward Father, his shirttail flying. Someone had shagged his shirt out. "I'll fotch it," Hig cried, stretching both hands for the key as a babe would reach.

"I'm not a-wanting it fotched," Father said. He'd not trust the key to a fellow who wasn't bright. "You've got it back'ards, Hig. I'm wanting it tuck."

Sill Lovelock stepped forward, though he didn't offer to carry the key. "They's Scripture ag'in' a feller hauling off the innocent," he vowed gravely. "I say, stay where there's a floor underfoot and joists overhead."

Father said testily, "There ought to be a statute telling a feller to salt his own steers. Ruther to drown o' sweat hunting for work than die o' dry rot in Hardstay."

Loss Tramble edged near Father, his eyes burning and the corners of his mouth curled. He nodded his head toward Sula Basham. "I'll deliver that key willing if you'll take this bean-pole widow-woman along some'eres and git her a man. She's wore the black bonnet long enough."

Laughter sprang forth, gulping in throats, wheezing noses. Sula whirled, her face lit with anger. "If I was a-mind to marry," she said, grudging her words, "it's certain I'd have to go where there's a man fitten. I'd be bound—"

Sill Lovelock broke in, thinking Sula's talk of no account. He asked Father, "What air you to use for bread along the way? There's no manna falling from Heaven this day and time."

Father was grinning at Sula. He saw the muscle knots clench on her arms, and he saw Loss inch away. He turned toward Sill in good humor. "Why, there's a gum o' honey dew on the leaves of a morning. We kin wake early and eat it off."

"The Devil take 'em," Mother said, calming Sula. "Men-folks are heathens. Let them crawl their own dirt." She was studying the locket, studying it to remember, to take away in her mind. I thought of Mother's unpierced ear lobes where never a bob had hung, the worn stems of her fingers never circled by gold, her plain bosom no pin-pretty had ever hooked. She was looking at the locket, not covetously, but in wonder.

"I'll take the key," Sula told Father. "Nobody else seems anxious to neighbor you."

Loss opened his hands, his face as grave as Sill Lovelock's, mocking. He pointed an arm at Sula, the other appealing to the crowd. "I allus did pity a widow-woman," he said. He spanned Sula's height with his eyes. "In this gethering there ought to be one single man willing to marry the Way Up Yonder Woman."

Sula's mouth hardened. "I want none o' your pity pie," she blurted. She took a step toward Loss, the sinews of her long arms quickening. When Loss retreated she turned to Mother, who had just climbed onto the wagon. Sula and Mother were now at an eye level. "You were a help when my chaps died," Sula said. "You were a comfort when my man lay in his box. I hain't forgetting. Wish I had a keepsake to give you, showing I'll allus remember."

"I'll keep you in my head," Mother assured.

"I'll be proud to know it."

We were ready to go. "Climb on, Son," Father called. I swung up from the hindgate to the top of the load. Over the heads of the men I could see the whole of the camp, the shotgun houses in the flat, the smoke rising above the burning gob heaps. The pain of leaving rose in my chest. Father clucked his tongue, and the mare started off. She walked clear out of the wagon shafts. Loose trace chains swung free and pole-ends of the shafts bounded to the ground.

"Whoa ho!" Father shouted, jumping down. A squall of joy sounded behind us. Cece Goodloe had pulled this rusty; he'd done the unfastening. Father smiled while adjusting the harness. Oh, he didn't mind a clever trick. And he sprang back onto the wagon again.

Loss Tramble spooled his hands, calling through them, "If you don't aim to take this widow along, we'll have to marry her to a born fool. We'll have to match her with Hig Sommers."

We drove away, the wheels taking the groove of ruts, the load swaying; we drove away with Sill Lovelock's last warning ringing our ears. "You're making your bed in Hell!" he had shouted. Then it was I saw the gold locket about Mother's neck, beating her bosom like a heart.

I looked back, seeing the first rocks thrown, hearing our

windows shatter; I looked back upon the camp as upon the face of the dead. I saw the crowd fall back from Sula Basham, tripping over each other. She had struck Loss Tramble with her fist, and he knelt before her, fearing to rise. And only Hig Sommers was watching us move away. He stood holding up his breeches, for someone had cut his galluses with a knife. He thrust one arm into the air, crying, "Hello, hello!"

# One Leg
# Gone to Judgment

IT was quiet on that day, and the willows hung limp over Troublesome Creek. The waters rested about the bald stones, scarcely moving. I had walked along the sandy left bank to Jute Dawson's homeseat, and in the soundlessness of afternoon young Clebe had not heard me enter the yard and climb the puncheon steps.

He sat at the end of the dogtrot with a rifle-gun sighted into the kitchen, his crutch leaning against a knee. His eyes were closed to a bead. I watched without speaking until he had fired, and the sound of a bullet striking pots and pans rang from the room.

Clebe hopped inside on his one leg, fetching out a fox squirrel by its grey brush. As he came out he saw me and held a quivering body aloft in greeting. There was a purple dent in the furred head, and red drops of blood trickled across the glassy eyes and twisted mouth. Clebe tossed the squirrel into a wooden bucket and hopped the length of the dogtrot for a chair.

"Fox squirrels are taking the place," he said. "We had a pet one and he drawed the rest out of the hills."

He laughed, his thin face spreading. "Nothing puts the lean in your muscles like squirrel gravy. When I spy a bowl of it on the table I have to clap my hand over my mouth to keep from shouting."

We settled into white-oak splint chairs and looked out on the untended patch before the house, now thick-growing with purple bonnets of stickweeds. Field sparrows were working among the slender stalks and the dark blossoms shook in the windless air.

"Poppy and Mommy are swapping work today," Clebe said. "Lukas Baldridge holp us lay-by our crap, and they're helping him stirring-off his sorghum to pay back. And I reckon they'll fetch us back a jug full of molasses."

Our chairs were leaned against the log framing and I sat there thinking of the wooden leg Jute had ordered for Clebe. The word had gone up and down Troublesome and its forks that a store-bought leg was coming for him, but the weeks had gone by and he had not been seen at either the horse swapping court, or the gingerbread election.

"I figure Lukas Baldridge is a clever man," Clebe said, "but Poppy says he's a straddle-pole of the worst kind. Poppy says he's got one foot that's a democrat and the other one a republican. And he can skip either direction, depending on who's handing out the money. He tuck a sled full of gingerbread to the last election and sold it near five times over to the candidates before he told folks to come and eat till they busted. He saw to it every candidate paid in."

The sparrows set up a clatter in the field patch. Their dull chirps were hollow and rasping, and their grey bodies blew dustily through the weeds.

"Even a sparrow-bird's got two wings," Clebe said at length, watching them work among the brown stalks. "A pure pity I hain't got two legs." He drew the palms of his hands tight and bloodless over the posts of the chair.

"Poppy ordered me a wood leg and it's an eternal time a-coming. A leg drummer come and measured me up careful. I reckon he counted every toe of mine and measured them before he got done, but I'm of a mind Poppy's been beat out of the fifty dollars he paid him. My opinion, he's tuck off like Snider's hound with Poppy's money.

"Oh, that fifty dollars will go hard with my pap if that leg don't come. If'n it don't, Poppy will shoot him till he looks like a rag doll does he ever get up with him. He'd had that money 'tater holed for a spell before he turned it loose."

Clebe drew a knife from his pocket and began to whittle the round of his chair. "Hit's been a heap of trouble I've give my Poppy," he said. "He was against the doc cutting off my leg when I had blood pizen but Mommy talked him to it. Aye, I can look up yonder on the point and see a yellow spot where I'd be buried now if they hadn't."

He stopped suddenly and pointed the blade at me. "I figure you never heard about the funeral occasion for my leg. Hit was buried just like folks are. My brother Tom fotched it from the doctor's house in a box and tuck it by the schoolhouse before books were called.

"All the scholars they come out to the road and looked at it. Before Tom left they were daring one another to touch it. They wanted to know what Tom was going to do with my limb, and Tom said he was going to have a real funeralizing on the point.

"The teacher he run Tom off because he couldn't get the scholars inside with my dead leg out there to look at. When he left, a bunch of the scholars tuck right along after him. They aimed to be in on anything that took place. They dug a hole right up yonder on the point. Well, now, Amos Morris preached the sermon and they tell me it was a scorcher. They tell me that if they was any devils around they'd a sneaked off with their forked tails between their legs. Then everybody took a last look and piled the dirt in.

"Then—you know what? Tom recollects that a fellow is liable to have the rheumatiz all the days of his life if his leg is buried with the toes a-curling. So up they dug my leg again and tried to pull the toes straight and they couldn't. What they done was to get rocks and beat the toes till they did straighten out. Tom done that for me. They buried the leg again and piled big flat rocks on the grave place to keep the dogs and varmints from scratching it up.

"O hit's a quare feeling to get one piece of you buried and gone to judgment before the rest of you dies. I'm afraid I might have a busted hard time getting myself together on resurrection day."

# The Quare Day

THERE had been no rain during the whole of August. At the month's end the winds came and blew through Little Angus valley, drying the creek to a shallow stream, and now it lay without motion like a long thin pond. Under the banks the waters were stained with shedding willow leaves. The wind had settled before the dew dried on the parched grass. Nothing stirred in the cool air pocketed in the damp hollows.

The sun was high above the hills when the sky beyond the ridge took on a yellow cast. There were no clouds other than a scattering of horsetails. At first the yellowness was only in the west, then it advanced, enveloping hilltop after hilltop until the sun-ball shone dully as through a saffron veil. It spread swiftly east, the hue of sulphur. It came without shape or sound bearing the molten glassiness of a sunset. Flaxbirds settled into the thickets. The dark hollow birds that warbled seldom in late summer sang not at all. Chickens went to an early roost in the sycamore trees, the prickly seed-balls hanging on twig-strings about their heads. They settled without sleeping, pale second lids opening and closing.

Shridy Middleton looked down the valley from the porch of her house. She polished her glasses with a fold of her sleeve and watched the yellow sand in the drying creek bed, the grey-yellow limestone shelved above the bank, the yellow-green of the chestnut oaks on the hills. She brushed her hands nervously over her hair, wondering at the color of the day. The mail hack had passed, and the wheels had rutted their tracks in the creek road. Willa Dowe, their neighbor's daughter, had brought a letter as she came to help with the apple drying, and now Shridy drew it out of her bosom, glancing curiously at the envelope without opening it. In a moment she thrust it back, brushed the meal dust from her apron, and stepped into the kitchen where Willa was paring apples.

"Hit's no use trying to dry fruit today," Shridy said. "The sun-ball has a mote in its eye. The slices would mold before they could cure." Willa was the same age as her son, Rein. Rein, the youngest of eleven, the most cherished, was the " 'possum baby," as the saying went. Willa and Rein had in infancy been cradled together when the families visited. To Shridy and her husband Jabe, Willa was the daughter they had hoped for but never had. Although related, the kinship was distant.

Willa stuck the knife into an apple as a holder and went to the door. She stood there a moment, rolling the plaits of her flaxen hair into a tight ball. She made a biscuit of it on her head. "As quare weather as ever I've seen," she remarked. "Mommy says fruit has to get direct sunlight or it'll lose sugar." Then, "I'd better get on down to home, for a bunch of things there need doing up." She paused in her leave-taking, recalling the letter. "But first I'll read what I brought from the mailbox. I'll say it to you and you can tell Uncle Jabe what's in it."

"The letter will keep until later," Shridy said, gathering the peelings into a basket for the chickens. "Hit'll endure till I set my mind to hear it."

Shridy watched her hurry along the path. Reaching the willows at the creek's bend, Willa began to run, her gingham dress flowing about her bare legs. When she had disappeared Shridy went around the house and peered up the hill toward the burned-over patch of new-ground on the second bench of the mountain. Jabe was leaning against a stump he had pulled with the help of his mule. He was staring toward the sun, hat in hand, and with no need to shade his eyes. The mule waited, brushing his nose over the charred earth.

Shridy called to him and the shrillness of her own voice rang in her ears. Jabe did not hear, her words being smothered by the redbud thicket between. She brought the fox horn from its nail by the mantel and blew into it with all her strength. Jabe turned and looked down, cupped his hands and blew an acknowledgement. Although it was not yet noon, he loosened the mule and started out of the field.

On coming from the barn Jabe heaped a turn of stovewood in his arms. Shridy met him on the porch. His face was butter-yellow like the air, his eyes the color of rain water drained from an oaken roof. And he noted her face, the sulphur hue of dry clay. Her hands appeared more leather than flesh.

"Hit's a plumb quare day," he said, going into the kitchen. "Must o' been a storm somewhere afar off to the west. My opinion, the wind has picked up dirt from a mighty spindling country where the ground is worn thin. Hain't the healthy kind like the wild dirt in my new-ground." He threw the turn of wood into the box beside the stove and kneeled to thrust splinters to quicken the coals.

"I'm baking an apple stack cake for dinner," she said, as if that were the reason for calling him in from his work.

Jabe arose slowly from his knees. "You're not baking a cake on Wednesday, shorely. We don't follow having Sunday cooking on Wednesday." He was puzzled. "Sort of uncommon, hain't it?"

She poured the stewed apples into a pan, and began to prepare batter for the layers. "Fruit won't dry on such a day," she explained. "Got to do something with the apples we've peeled." The letter was like a stone in her dress bosom.

Standing in the doorway, leaning against the jamb, Jabe viewed the ragweeds marching along the fencerow of the meadow. They seemed yellow as bolted mustard. A golden carpet spread across the pasture which had been lately mowed.

Shridy called to Jabe from the stove, "You ought to put on a clean shirt if we're to have apple stack cake for dinner. Hit's sort of an occasion." Jabe went into the front room, closed the door and pulled the latch-string inside. He lifted the great Bible from the maple highboy. It was weighty and he sat down and opened it upon his lap. The pages turned familiarly under his hard thumb. He squinted along the double columns, leafing slowly through the chapters, pausing to scan the revelations and miracles. Every page knew his finger, every sentence his eye. The Book was the herald of the past, the prophecy of the future. After a spell he put the Book away, washed himself and donned a fresh shirt.

The sun was poised overhead when he returned. Dinner was spread upon the table. The pole beans, the salt pork, the beet pickles and sliced onions were in the new dishes Rein had sent from Ohio in the spring. The cornbread on its flowered platter was as golden as the day itself. The tablecloth had come from Rein's wife whom they had never seen. They stood by the table and studied the dishes, rimmed with laurel buds. The linen tablecloth was stark white, cold and strange; it was as if the plates rested on snow. Unspoken were the words that Willa had read to them from the note pinned to it when it arrived: *To my dear Father and Mother.*

Jabe and Shridy were uneasy about the note which expressed a warmth they did not feel, sent by one they had yet to know. They had weighed the words, looking startled and speechless into each other's eyes. This was Rein's wife, their daughter-in-law, they kept reminding themselves. The spouse of their son's choosing. But she was not their choice. They had chosen Willa, had counted on his return to claim her. But they must acknowledge Rein's woman, accept her, stranger though she be.

Rein's wife had written a letter after their marriage in June; in July there was another in her small, slanted script. There was none of Rein's stubby scrawling on the pages. Willa had read the letters aloud, for Shridy could not read and handwriting confused Jabe. They had listened quietly. After the second letter Shridy had spoken her fear. "Be it Rein doesn't write the next time, hit's a sure sign his wife is going to do all the talking from now till Kingdom Come. He'll be lost to us."

Jabe drew back his chair and sat down. "We oughten to put these dishes away and just use 'em for company," he said. "They won't wear out before we're gone from the world. They're from him, recollect." Shridy's eyes followed the long pattern of the tablecloth as she sank into her chair and folded her hands into a knot in her lap. The letter with the small, slanted script was like a scorpion in her bosom.

In mid-afternoon they sat upon the front porch. The sun had swollen above the hills and now its yellow mask shone dull as hammered metal. The hound's breathing came up through the puncheon floor in moist gasps. There was no movement along the creekbed road. Nothing except the mail hack had passed during the day. The silence and the yellowness swallowed the valley. A jar-fly fiddled in the maple shading the yard and buttery croaks of a frog sounded from the meadow.

"Hit takes a day like this to bresh up the mind and keep us beholden to the Almighty," Jabe said. "Not many of them as gilded as His throne He lets us see in our day and time."

Shridy swung back and forth in her rockingchair, her right hand resting upon her bosom. When it seemed the letter would jump out of itself she drew it forth and held it out to Jabe. "It's from them," she said.

Jabe jerked toward her. "Who writ it?" he asked impatiently.

"Hit's from her," Shridy said. Jabe sank back into his seat in sudden weariness. His hands clenched the chairposts.

The cows began to gather at the pasture gate. They waited without lowing. Jabe rose slowly from his chair and walked toward the barn. The path curved among the hillocks of earth, running before him into the hills. Little Angus Creek was molten gold. Not a wing stirred in the yellow air.

# The Fun Fox

THE day I opened the Keg Branch School I rolled my sleeves to display my muscles, and I kept a pointing-stick handy.

Keg Branch was in the upper part of the county—'the jumping-off-place,' some folk call it. The highway played out miles this side, and the creek bed served as the road. The behavior at the school was notorious; but I was eighteen, anxious to undertake my first teaching job, and the Keg Branch position was the only one open.

The superintendent of county schools had given me ample warning. "All sorts of chicanery will be attempted," he had said, "even to riding you on a rail. Yet my rule is: a rail ride is a discharge, for a teacher must stay master. And an old citizen may plague this term—one I angered by my refusal to authorize a new schoolhouse. The building is in bad condition, I'm bound to admit. Still, I'll not sanction another until the children mend their ways. He swore he'd bring a fool's look to somebody's face."

"The children won't wrap me around their thumbs," I had boasted, "and I'll get at the root of the trouble. I'll stand shy of the old fellow."

"They've run off even experienced teachers," the superintendent had explained, "but I feel I should give you a trial, in spite of my doubt you can last. Prove me wrong if you can, and hang on at least until I find a substitute."

The surprise that greeted me when I arrived on Keg Branch took me aback. The schoolhouse was brand-new! It sat on the foundation of the old one, upon a wedge of land between a cliff and a swamp and the creek, with scarcely space, as the saying goes, to swing a hungry cat. My surprise was so great that the lack of a playground didn't strike me at once. At Argus Bagley's where the teacher customarily lodged, I expressed my astonishment over the building.

Argus explained, "Up until a few sessions ago, the discipline of the scholars was fair, but for some reason it worsened. They've turned the school into a hurrah's nest. We rebuilt in the expectation it might improve matters."

I inquired, "Why was it done without the county's support and knowledge?"

Argus chuckled. "Ever hear of Mace Crownover?"

I shook my head, wondering.

"Well, you're in his territory," Argus said. "The new building was his notion, and when the superintendent refused to help, the community humored Mace by providing lumber and labor. What Mace wants he usually gets."

Then I knew. "I've heard mention of Crownover," I said. "He's got the superintendent fooled, certainly."

"Confounding folks is Old Mace's trade," Argus said. "What that fun fox will do is beyond guessing. Still, he's not so feisty as he used to be, not so ready with pranking and telling tales. Declares his wife is beginning to draw a tight rein and that he's on the borders of swearing off tricks and tales for life. No matter. If ever you cross his path, keep your eyes skinned."

"I understand he's apt to make my job the harder," I said.

"Oh, I reckon not," Argus said. "Yet I doubt he'd let pass a chance to hocus any person. Always up to mischief, that's his history. Why, right now he has a forty-dollar collect package in the post office and he vows he'll clear it. He'll clear it, says he, and I'd swear he hasn't a cent to his pocket. A trick, I'd bet my ears."

"What does the package contain?" I inquired, mildly curious.

Argus grinned. "He says it's for him to know and for us to find out."

Forty-eight children, ranging in age from six to sixteen, from tads in the primer to overgrown eighth-graders, attended school the first day, and they came with eyes gleaming. They acted as I'd been told to expect. Spitballs rained, erasers zoomed, tricks were rife. Antics were pulled under my very nose, though catch a body I could not. Unwittingly I wore a sign on my back: "Hello the rabbit!" They laughed when I flexed my arms, when I whistled the pointing-stick, when I threatened or scolded. A good thing Mace Crownover didn't show up, for I already had my hands full.

The next day, I learned I was truly in for a bug race. A chair collapsed under me, soot blackened my fingers when I reached into a crayon box, the pointing-stick broke when I lifted it. Wasps in my lunch basket stung me, and the water in the well turned inky.

Again I caught nobody at mischief—none save a primer child sewing together the pockets of a coat I'd hung on a peg. Bad deportment to the contrary, the children were eager and bright at their studies, and they were respectful toward the new building, neither marking nor scarring it. At recess and at noon they jostled in the small area before the door. There was no room for even marble games or hopscotch, and I gazed covetously at Argus Bagley's posted land across the creek. Argus was the principal landowner in the section.

They kept me walking on pencils the week long, and such was my torment I almost forgot about Mace Crownover. Thorns were in my chair, cockleburs in my pockets, a fresh bouquet of sneezeweeds atop my desk daily. My hat was regularly glued to the wall, and a greased plank sprawled me twice. Yet the scamps were cunning enough to escape detection.

However, on Thursday afternoon I found a clue to their misbehavior. A student read a theme, which began: "A man bought a horse off Mace Crownover. The critter was blue or green or purple. You couldn't tell which. You couldn't learn till rain washed away the pokeberry and madder dye. The beast was gray. Gray as teeth."

The children listened, eyes round and mouths ajar. At the completion one said, "Old Mace's tricks are the best a-going."

And another chirruped, "Ought to hear him taletell. He can spin them from now till Sunday, and every word the truth."

I thought, Ah-ha, so it's Crownover's example they're following. I hushed them abruptly and would permit no further mention of him. The children took it ill. They batted their eyes at each other and closed their textbooks with a snap. They acted as though the final day of the term had come.

And Friday morning, on opening the door, I discovered a fence rail leaning in a corner.

I knew by now I couldn't fend off four-dozen children. The eighth-graders alone could handle me. But come what may, I'd not surrender without a tussle. I'd stick till the last pea hopped out of the pod. I ignored the rail, feigning not to see it, and I schemed to delay the reckoning. I conducted a three-hour spelling bee—spelling was their delight. I skipped recess and held the lunch period indoors, in the meantime reading to them from *Tom Sawyer*. I read all afternoon, and they could not tear their ears away. Thus I squeezed through till closing.

In the evening, while I was cudgeling my mind to decide what to do Monday, Argus brought a message. He reported: "Old Mace announces he'll clear the package at the post office tomorrow, and he's inviting the doubters to come witness it. Says he wants the schoolteacher there in particular."

I replied bitterly, "He's setting the stage for a hoax."

Argus chuckled, "That fox would saw off a toe for a laugh. He's the cat's beard."

"In my opinion," I blurted, "he's the downfall of the Keg Branch School."

Argus jerked his chin, surprised at my accusation, and he defended Crownover. "Had it not been for him, you'd be teaching in a shack," he said. "Squirrels used to steal the lunches through the cracks. Come a high wind, shingles scattered like leaves. Walk the floor, you made a noise like a nest of crickets."

To argue would serve no purpose, I decided. I smothered my rancor and said, "The package doesn't concern me."

"A trick, naturally," Argus said, "and he may pull it on you. Nevertheless, be on hand and show you're not bluffed out. Remember that courage goes a long way in this community."

Though tempted, I said, "I've borne enough misdoings for one week."

"Humor the old gent," Argus advised. "I'll go along and start him talking so he won't rack you too heavy. Go, and count it a part of your education."

The post office occupied a corner of the general store just above the schoolhouse. Saturday morning early, when Argus and I arrived, the counters and feed bags and barrels were covered with men, and the crowd overflowed onto the porch. Argus found a seat on a sack of salt, and Zack Tate, postmaster and merchant, furnished a crate for me to sit on. A stool stood bare, awaiting Mace.

Argus proposed to Zack, "Let's try loosening Mace's tongue. Before he locks his lips absolutely, we ought to hear him relate one more tale."

Zack agreed. "Say we do. We'll try, though it seems nowadays his wife has him twisted down tighter'n a nut on a bolt."

The crowd smiled expectantly.

"You believe he'll have money enough to free the package?" someone asked.

Zack said, "He's just wagging you fellers. Haven't you learned that?"

"I know him well enough not to read him off too quick," came the reply.

A man inquired, "Anybody made a reasonable guess what's in the bundle?"

"Maybe the devil's eyeteeth," a joker said.

Time passed. Eight o'clock came without a glimpse of Mace. At eight-thirty, the mail rider reported he'd seen nobody along the creek road. By nine, the men had become restless.

To hold them, Argus said, "Mace is giving the crowd a while to swarm and will appear right shortly."

Right as a rabbit's foot! It wasn't long before a cry arose outside. "Yonder comes Old Scratch!" And presently Mace was standing in the doorway. The walk had winded him, and he was panting. He was about sixty-five years of age, wide-faced and bushy-browed. His eyes were as blue as a marsh wren's eggs in a ball of grass.

Argus shoved the post office stool forward, greeting, "You're late, Old Buddy. Sit and rest and give an account of yourself."

"I promised my wife I'd do my duty and hurry home," Mace answered. He scanned the crowd, his gaze settling on me.

"What antic delayed you?" Argus baited. "Confess up."

"Why, I'm a changed character," Mace snorted. He accepted the offered seat, still looking in my direction. When he'd regained his breath he addressed me, "I figure you're the new teacher."

I nodded coldly.

"I'm hoping to thresh out and settle a matter today," he spoke gravely.

Zack Tate broke in, "The package is ready any time you are, Mace."

"It'll preserve an extra minute," Mace replied.

Argus caught his chance. "Tell us a big one while you rest. Tell of the occasion you turned the tables on the town barber after he'd short-shaved you."

Mace jerked his head as if slapped. "Never in life has a razor touched my jaws."

"You singe them off, aye?"

"Now, no," Mace said. "I climb a tree, tie my whiskers to a limb, and jump out." While the crowd guffawed, he pinned me with a stern glare and said, "The word comes the scholars are running you bowlegged. Still, their behavior has improved mightily over last session. Not a window broken, not a desk whittled, not a peephole drilled through the walls."

Argus spoke quickly to draw Mace's attention. "Come on and relate some rusty you've pulled and we'll not bother you more. You be the chooser. Anything."

Mace's eyes sparkled despite himself. "Let me name the word 'rusty' and my woman will wring my neck. And remember, I'm trying to conquer my trifling."

The men batted eyes at each other. Mace was a slick hand at double talk.

"Ah, quit stalling," Argus begged. "Tell of the foot logs you doctored to snap in two under people, the gallus straps cut during election rallies, the 'dumb-bulls' you fashioned to stampede cattle. Or tell of you dying—playing stone dead purely to hear your kin hallo and bawl."

But Mace would not. He went on talking to me. "I decided last spring, if matters rode unhindered, the Keg Branch children would grow into bad citizens."

"Hark! Hark!" Zack Tate cried.

"Somebody had to take hold of the problem," Mace said, "and I did. I took to spying on other schools to learn why ours didn't prosper. It boiled down to a couple of needs: a new schoolhouse, and a collection of stuff. The schoolhouse is built. Lastly, the stuff's here."

The crowd smirked.

Mace rose, hat in hand. "You know me, my friends, and

surely you don't want your young'uns marching in my tracks. You have a chance to straighten them out, so unknot your money sacks and give till it pinches." He held his hat brim up, dug a half-dollar from his pocket, and dropped it in. At sight of the coin, both Zack and Argus gasped.

"What's in the bundle?" a complaint sounded. "We're buying a pig in a poke."

"Don't you trust me?" asked Mace.

"Gee-o, no!" was the reply.

"Well, my wife doesn't either," Mace sighed. "The reason I've got to hurry." He passed the hat, cajoling and pleading. "Cough up, you tightwads, you eagle chokers. Forty dollars will buy peace. And recollect it's in your children's behalf."

None took Mace seriously, though most were willing to help the prank along. They flung money into the hat and laughed.

But to Argus, who shucked loose a dollar bill, Mace said, "We'll not accept a penny from you."

Argus was puzzled. "My money will spend the same as the next person's," he said.

"Hold your 'tater," Mace said, "and directly I'll tell what you're assessed. You're to give the most."

"Huh!" grunted Argus in bafflement.

When it appeared the last dime had been bled out of the crowd, the money was counted. It lacked ninety cents of reaching the full amount.

Argus offered, "I'll finish the pot."

Mace shook his head.

Zack volunteered, "Mace, I'll throw in the remainder if you'll agree to one simple thing."

"Say on," bade Mace.

"Confess how you came by your half-dollar."

"You wouldn't believe the truth, did you hear it."

"Speak it, and I'll try."

Mace squirmed on the stool. He moaned, "I oughten to throw away a precious secret. After you know, you'll all follow the practice, and money will get too common. It won't buy dirt."

"Tell and be done."

"I hate to."

"We're listening."

Mace yielded grudgingly. "Fetching that fifty-cent piece was the cause of my tardiness," he said. "I had to travel clear to the breaks of the mountains to upturn a rock I'd spit under six months ago. A pity I couldn't have waited a year. By then it would have grown to a dollar."

The package was brought. The crowd moved warily aside as Mace unclasped his knife, thrust the handle toward Zack, and said, "Cut the twine and open it."

"Aye, no," Zack refused. "Someone else can play the goat."

"Upon my word and deed and honor!" Mace blared. "Do you think it's full of snakes?"

"It's untelling," Zack said.

Mace appealed to Argus. "Open it quick. I'm bound to hustle."

"Scared to," Argus replied honestly.

Mace lifted his hands in sorrow. He groaned, "I've come on a bitter day. I've totally lost the confidence of my fellow-man." As he spoke, he moved toward me, proffering the knife. "Here," he said, "prove I'm not a false speaker."

I shrugged. I'd as lief as not. Hadn't Argus said courage was honored on Keg Branch? I accepted the knife, and mouths in the crowd stretched to laugh. I cut the twine and broke the wrappings, and out rolled a volley ball, a basketball, baseballs, nets, and bats.

As we blinked Mace told Argus, "You're to donate the playground—a piece of the land you own across from the schoolhouse. The scholars need elbow room to burn up their surplus energy."

All stared in wonder, but mine was the only face that bore a fool's look.

Mace clapped on his hat and strode toward the door. At the threshold he glanced round, his eyes shining. "I'm going home and tell my wife to skin me alive for mixing in sorry company."

It turned out that I taught through the entire session on Keg Branch—and two more besides.

# The Run
# for the Elbertas

*A*S Riar Thomas approached the Snag Fork bridge, the truck lights picked up the two boys sitting on the head wall. Glancing at his watch, he saw it was nearly one o'clock. He halted, pulled the cardboard out of the broken window, and called, "I'll open the door from the inside, it's cranky." The boys sat unmoving. "Let's go," he said, "if you're traveling with me. A body can't fiddle in the peach business."

Godey Spurlock began honing his knife on the concrete, and Mal Dowe got his out too. "Pay us before we start," Godey said. "We hain't going to be slicked."

"What I say," said Mal.

"My grabbies!" Riar chuffed. "You ever know me hiring anybody and failing to settle?"

"They tell you trade out of paying," Godey said. "People didn't name you 'Tightwad' for nothing." Yet it wasn't the money that made Godey stall. He was angling to help drive.

Mal said, "Doss and Wint Colley claim you skinned them the last trip."

Riar snapped the clutch in irritation. "Nowadays," he snorted, "you can hear everything but the truth and the meat a-frying." And he said, "Why do you think I take my own help? To see I get the fruit I buy. Doss and Wint let the loaders short me a dozen bushels. Still I paid off."

"Yeah," said Godey, "in rotten peaches."

"I've tried several fellers," Riar explained, "and the shed

crews stole them blind. I need fellers sharp to the thieves. They can trick you and you looking at them."

"Not us they can't," Godey said. "We hain't lived sixteen years for nothing." He slid from the head wall, and Mal followed. "Settle now and we'll guarantee you full measure."

"You know us," said Mal.

"Never in life have I paid for work before it was done," Riar declared, "and I don't aim to begin." He waited. "Are you going or not? Make up your heads."

Edging toward the truck, Godey said, "Promise to let me drive a dab, and we'll risk you."

"Risk me," Riar hooted, slapping the wheel. "If there's another person who'd undertake hauling you jaspers from Kentucky to South Carolina and back I haven't met the witty."

Godey insisted, "Do I get to steer after a while?"

Riar raced the engine impatiently, and the cattle rack clattered behind. "Crawl in," he said, "I can't fool. To deal in ripe peaches and come out you've got to run for them. It's a five-hundred-mile round trip, and I'll have to get there in plenty of time to make arrangements and load by sundown. We've got a splinter of Virginia to cross, a corner of Tennessee, and North Carolina top to bottom."

"I'll give you my knife to drive a speck. It has four blades and all kinds of tricks and things."

Riar shook his head. "I'm gone."

Godey saw Riar meant it and they got in. He warned Riar, "Anybody who beats us will be a-hurting." And he said, "If you want to keep me acting pretty you'd better give me the wheel along the way."

"Now, yes," echoed Mal.

Though it was July the night was chilly. Riar said, "Stuff the board in the window or you'll get aired."

"I'll not ride blind," Godey said.

"When you begin freezing," said Riar, "don't halloo to me."

Mal said, "Let me sit on the board. They's a spring sticking me through the cushion."

Godey laughed. "That makes it mean," he said, and he sat upon the cardboard himself. The truck sputtered in starting, and he teased Riar, "What about a feller who'd hang on to a wreck?"

"She'll run like a sewing machine in a minute," Riar said.

"Too stingy to buy a new, aye? Can't say farewell to a dollar."

Riar said, "You knotheads know the cost of a truck? They'll bankrupt you."

"The fashion you scrimp, you ought to be rich as Jay Goo."

Riar grunted. "Boys don't understand beans," he said, and in his truck's defense, "I've had her repaired for the trip, though I couldn't afford it: brakes relined, spark plugs changed, retreads all round."

"Yeah," Godey ridiculed. "Fenders flopping, windows cracked out. A bunch of screaks and rattles."

"We heard your old gee-haw four miles away," added Mal.

Riar said, "Doubt you not, she'll carry us there and fetch us back—with two hundred bushels of peaches." And he mused, "I used to mule in goods from Jackson. Occasionally my wagon would break down and I couldn't fix it. I'd walk up the road and 'gin to whistle. Fairly soon it would come to me what to do."

"My opinion," said Godey, "the most you calculate on is how to dodge spending money."

"Listen," Riar said gravely, "I've barely my neck above water. Bought the tires on credit, went into debt for repairs. I'll have to make a killing this run to breathe. And if I am a grain thrifty it's on behalf of my family."

"They say," plagued Mal, "you're married to the woman on the silver dollar."

"Let me give you some gospel facts," said Riar.

"We can bear it if you can spare it," sang Godey.

"I try to keep bread on the table and shoes on my young'uns' feet. And I treat the other feller square. I'm straight as an icicle."

"What about the rotten peaches you put off on Doss and Wint Colley?" reminded Godey. "Preach a sermon on that."

"The fruit at the bottom of the load was mashed shapeless and beginning to spoil," said Riar, "yet the Colleys asked for them instead of pay. Claimed they wanted to plant the seeds and commence an orchard."

"Idjits might swallow that tale," said Godey, "but not us. You believe yourself they actually wanted the seeds?"

"I've come on different knowledge since."

"For what? Tell me."

"You won't hear it from me."

Mal saw light suddenly. "Just one thing they could of done—made peach brandy."

"You reckon?" blurted Godey, his ire rising. "Lied to skip giving us a taste?"

"It's plain as yore nose," said Mal.

"By jacks," Godey huffed, "we'll work on their dog hides."

"What's the profit in revenge?" Riar chided. "Swapping ill with your fellow man?"

"You don't know?" asked Godey in mock surprise.

"No," said Riar.

"Then I'll tell you. It makes you feel a whole heap better."

Mal asked Riar, "Don't you ever get mad and fly off the hinges?"

"I try to control myself," said Riar. And he advised, "You two ought to get some sleep. We'll have no pull-offs for naps along the road."

Mal twisted on the cushion. "Upon my honor," he grumbled, "this seat is eating my breeches up."

Morning found them in the Holston Valley of Tennessee, and the sun got busy early. The moment the ground mist melted, it was hot. The truck was standing at a gasoline pump, the attendant hose in hand and inquiring, "How many?" when Godey woke. Godey's eyes flew open. He said, "Fill her up to the wormholes."

"Five gallons," said Riar.

Godey yawned, bestirring Mal. He said, "I never slept me nary a wink last night."

"Me neither," fibbed Mal.

"You snore just to make the music, aye?" said Riar. "It was hookety-hook between you."

Godey said, "Why don't you fill the tank and not have to stop at every pig track?"

"Ever hear of evaporation?" asked Riar. "A lot goes away before you can burn it."

Godey wagged his head. "Tight as Dick's hatband," he informed the attendant.

Mal said, "Saving as a squirrel."

Directly they were on the road, Godey announced, "I'm hungry, Big Buddy, and what are you going to do about it?"

"We're carrying food the wife prepared," Riar said. "We'll halt at the next black spot."

"You expect to feed us stale victuals?" Godey complained. "Give us a quarter apiece to buy hamburgers."

Riar said, "During my boy days a quarter looked big as a churn lid. Did a body have one he stored it. Now all the young understand is to pitch and throw."

"The truth," mocked Godey. "Saturday I was in town, and I hadn't been there ten minutes when bang went a dime."

"We have food in plenty, I tell you," Riar insisted, "and any we don't use will be wasted."

"So that's the hitch," scoffed Godey. "Before I'd live like you I'd whittle me a bill and peck amongst the chickens."

Riar halted presently in the shade of a beech and hurried out. Mal forced the cranky door on his side and jumped to the ground, and Godey made to pile after—but his breeches caught on the spring. He pulled and still hung. He had to jerk

loose. His jaws paled, his mouth twisted to swear, yet he
checked himself. He would make it pay later. He hopped
down, and none was the wiser.

Mal cautioned Godey under his breath, "You'd better
begin greasing Riar up if you're expecting to drive."

"I've already got him right where I want him," said
Godey.

Riar put a gunny sack on the grass and spread breakfast:
saucer-size biscuits, fried ribs, a wedge of butter. He poured
cold coffee from a mason jar into cups shorn of handles.

Godey eyed the meal sourly, keeping turned to hide the
rip. "A dog wouldn't eat a mess like that," he caviled. Nevertheless he took a serving. With cheeks full he added, "I
wouldn't except I'm so weak I couldn't rattle dry leaves."

"You might do as well at your own table," Riar countered, "but it's not my information."

Hardly were they moving again than Godey broached
driving. "I'm ready to steer awhile, Big Buddy."

Riar grunted noncommittally.

"Last night you let on I could."

"I never made such talk. I promised you two dollars, and
have them you will the moment they're earned."

Godey produced his knife. "I'll give you this, and hit's a
bargain. Four regular blades, and an awl, and a punch, and a
shoe hook, and—"

"All that play-daddle is fit for is to rub a hole in your
pocket."

"Then," said Godey determinedly, "I'm going to have
my wages now, cash on the barrel."

"Are you making that cry again?" fretted Riar. "They
said you were pranky, but I didn't figure on all the mouth I'm
having to put up with."

"You heard me."

"My opinion," Mal joined in, "you're not to be confi-
denced."

Godey declared, "Fork over else we'll allow the shed
crews to steal you ragged. Even might help 'em."

"Great sakes!" Riar exclaimed. "Two dollars not yours yet and you growling for them."

"Why, you're behind the times," corrected Godey. "You're paying me an extra three to buy a pair of breeches. Your old cushion has tore a hole in me big as outdoors."

Riar sputtered, "I haven't taken you to raise, Mister Boy."

"According to law," said Godey, displaying the tear, "I've suffered damage in your vehicle. I know my rights."

"I'll see you to a needle and thread."

Godey had Riar going, and he knew it. He said cockily, "Want to satisfy me and not have to tip your pocketbook?"

"Deliver my life and living into your hands?" Riar chuffed, on to the proposition.

"Turn the truck over to me thirty minutes and I'll forget the breeches. I may even decide to let you off paying me for a while."

Riar groaned. "My young'uns' bread depends on this machine." But he was tempted. Loading without watchers was a misery, and he couldn't abide further expense.

"It's me drive," Godey said, "or you shell out five dollars."

"Wreck my truck," Riar bumbled, "and I'm ruined. You don't care." But he could see no alternative. "I get along with folks if they'll let me," he said, relenting. And he questioned anxiously, "Will you stay on your side of the road and run steady and not attempt to make an airplane of it?"

"Try me."

Riar slowed and stopped, and he took pliers and bent the point of the broken spring. Godey slid under the wheel, face bright with triumph, and he asked, "Anything coming behind?"

The truck moved away evenly, the gears knuckling without sound. Watch in hand, Riar prompted, "Don't ride the clutch," and "She's not tied up for speed," and "She brakes on the three-quarter pedal." But his coaching was useless, as Godey drove well enough.

Meeting a bus, Godey poked his head out and bawled, "Get over, Joab," and he grumbled, "Some people take their part of the highway in the middle." He reproved Riar. "Why don't you quit worrying. You make a feller nervous."

"I can't," breathed Riar. "Not for my life."

Before Godey's half hour was through he inquired, "Have I done to suit you?"

"You'll get by," grudged Riar.

"How far to the North Carolina line?"

"Another hour should fetch it."

Godey's eyes narrowed. "Want to pet your pocketbook again?"

"What now?" Riar asked skeptically.

"I've decided to swap my pay to drive to there."

"You're agreeing to pass up the money, aye? And after vilifying me about the Colley brothers."

"I aim to," said Godey, "and I won't argue."

Riar shook his head. "I promised cash, and cash you'll have. I'll prove to you June bugs my word is worth one hundred cents to the dollar."

Godey shrugged. "Made up your mind, Big Buddy?"

"Absolutely."

"Well," said Godey, "let's see can we change it," and without further ado he floored the accelerator. The truck jumped, the cattle rack leapt in the brackets. The shovel hanging from the slats thumped the cab.

"Scratch gravel," crowed Mal. "Pour on the carbide."

"Mercy sakes!" croaked Riar.

Godey spun the wheel back and forth. He zig-zagged the road like a black snake. The rack swayed, threatening to break free.

Riar's mouth opened, but nothing came out. The veins on his neck corded.

Godey cut to the left side of the highway and sped around a blind curve.

Riar could stand no more. "All right," he gasped. "All right."

Godey slackened. Grinning he said, "Why, you break your word fairly easy. Get you up against it and you'll breach."

By early afternoon they had put western North Carolina behind and crossed into South Carolina. The mountains fell back, the earth leveled and reddened, the first peach orchards came to view. The sun beat down, and the cab was baking hot.

Riar charged the boys, "I'm expecting you to keep your eyes skinned when they load my peaches. The fruit goes on several bushels together, and the sharpers can trip you."

Godey and Mal sniggered. Godey said, "Did they know it, it's us they'd better watch."

"What I say," agreed Mal.

"I'm after my honest due," Riar said. "I don't intend to cheat or be cheated." And a thought seized him. Glancing swiftly at the boys he said, "You can count to two hundred, I hope to my soul."

"I can count my finger," jested Godey.

"How much schooling have you had?"

"Aye," said Godey, "I learned who killed Cock Robin."

Mal said, "Godey Spurlock coming up short hain't been heard of."

Beyond Landrum a packing house appeared, the metal roof glaring sunlight. Riar drove past, and Godey clamored, "Hain't you going to stop?"

"They're a contract outfit," Riar said. "They wax and shine their fruits like a pair of Sunday shoes, and some retail at ten cents apiece. They don't deal with the little feller."

"They'd allow us to peep around, I reckon."

To humor them, Riar drew in at the next shed. "Another large operator," he explained, "and we won't buy here either. Just stretch our legs and cool."

A line of ten-wheel trucks was parked at the loading platform, and Godey breathed, "Gee-o! Look at the big jobs." He teased Riar. "Hain't you ashamed to take your old plug out where people can see it?"

"Not in the least," said Riar.

From the platform Godey and Mal gazed under the shed. They saw the roll conveyors tumbling fruit forward, the workers busy at the picking belts. Hail-pecked and wormy fruits were being shunted aside. The peaches flowed on through sizers and brushes of the defuzzer to the packers, and there seemed no end to them.

Godey's eye lit on a huge peach in a basket, and he snatched it up. A voice behind him spoke, "You're welcome, young fellow, stuff till you bust." Without deigning to turn, Godey held out the great peach and sneered "Pea-jibbit!" and let it fall and stepped on it. But he peeled and ate six others.

When Riar got up with the boys twenty minutes later there was nothing they had not looked at. As they drove away Godey said, "The first ever I knowed peaches have hairs like cats."

"Get them brushings on you," said Riar, "and they'll eat you alive."

"What they told me," said Godey. "Claimed it takes a spell to dig in, but after it does bull nettles hain't a patching to it."

Said Mal, "We'd got some, did we have a poke to put 'em in."

"Of what use is it? I ask you."

Said Godey, "For Doss and Wint Colley a beating is too fine. I want to see them dance."

"Now, yes," said Mal. "They'd throw an ague fit."

Riar frowned. "Hitting back at folks is all you think of."

Two miles beyond Landrum, Riar turned onto a dirt road and the wheels set the dust boiling. The boys' faces were streaked where they wiped the sweat. Riar stopped at a number of small-growers' sheds, buying at none, saying, "They sell high as Haman," or "Their fruit is too green for my business," or "Most of my customers want Elbertas."

Godey said, "Always I've heard a fruit bought off of you had better be stomached quick, it's so rotty-ripe."

"The mellower the cheaper," said Riar.

Mal said, "You'll travel farther for a dollar than anybody on creation."

"Was I you," said Godey, "I'd take any peaches handy and call 'em Elbertas, and nobody'd know the difference."

Riar shook his head. "When I say a thing is such and such, you can count on it."

"Oh, yes?" scoffed Godey. "You point me to a plumb honest feller, and I'll show you a patch of hair growing in the palm of his hand."

"My opinion," gibed Mal, "He's hunting a place where they give away."

"About the size of it," said Godey.

"Even if I had my fruit on order I'd wait until the shade comes over," said Riar. "I don't cook my peaches by hauling in the sun."

The shed where Riar bought was a barn with the sides gone. A single processing unit was operated by the owner's family, and the picking belt was lined with children. Elbertas and Georgia Belles and J. H. Hales lay across the floor in drifts.

With Godey and Mal at his heels Riar inspected the heaps. Encountering a boy, Godey opened his knife and greeted, "Hello, Coot, what'll you give to boot?" He lifted a Georgia Belle on the awl, peeled it with the butcher blade, used the shoe hook to pluck the seed. A second youngster hastened to watch, and Godey readied another, bringing the scalper and corkscrew into play.

The owner cast an appraising look at Riar. Noting his eye on a section of Elbertas three days harvested he said, "There's your bargain. A dollar and a quarter a bushel." To explain their being on hand he added, "The whole crop is trying to shape up the same minute."

Riar broke several in half. The flesh was grainy and yellow. He tasted, and they had the sugar. Though much softer than he usually handled, he judged most could bear the trip. They would last the night and the cool of the morning. If he bought them reasonably and peddled them at two fifty, he could clear his debts and have money left. What matter the loss of the bottom layers. He said, "I'll pay seventy cents."

The owner had hardly expected to get rid of the aging fruit. Still he said, "I can't accept less than a dollar."

"Seventy cents," repeated Riar.

"Yesterday they were a dollar fifty."

"Day after tomorrow," parried Riar, "you'll have to scrape them up."

Godey butted in. "People don't call him Tightwad just to beat their gums."

Riar's neck reddened, but he held himself.

Trying to make a stand, the owner said, "I'll drop to eighty, but they'll rot on the floor before I'll accept less."

"Well, then," said Riar, "we can't do business, for I won't pay above seventy for dead-ripe peaches." Shuffling to go he asked, "How far to the next shed?"

The owner changed his tune. He said, "Couldn't we split the difference and meet in the middle?"

Riar gazed at the Elbertas. Only hovering gnats bespoke their advanced maturity. "I'll tell you what I will do," he proposed, "and we can both keep our word. I'll pay eighty for a hundred and seventy-five bushels if you'll throw in the twenty-five that are bound to mash."

"Riar to a whisker," said Godey.

After figuring a moment, the owner grumbled, "But you'd still be getting them at seventy cents."

"What I know," admitted Riar.

Throwing up his arms, the owner groaned, "Take 'em, take 'em."

The sun was still high. Leaving Godey and Mal on their own, Riar rested in the truck, but it was too sultry to sleep. And at sunset he called them with, "My peaches will never be any greener." Godey carried a paper poke, the neck of which was tied with string, and Riar said, "If that's something you've picked up, leave it lay."

"Where I go this poke goes," said Godey.

Guessing the contents, Riar said, "The stuff will not ride in the cab with me." Yet thinking to forbear until he had his peaches aboard, he added, "If you're so set on it, put the poke in the toolbox." He figured to lose it later.

The children loaded the truck, the smaller filling baskets and sending by conveyor to the platform, the larger hoisting them over the rack and emptying. The work quickened upon the arrival of a contract van. Riar counted at the tail gate, and Godey and Mal clung to the slats and sang out the number, and though three measures were often dumped at a time, Riar got his two hundred without a doubt.

The servicing of the van started immediately. And the moment Riar and the owner disappeared into the crib office to settle up, Godey traded his knife to the boys. Five bushels of Georgia Belles headed for the van were switched onto Riar's truck.

At leaving, Riar handed Mal two dollars and advised, "Keep them in your pocket, they won't spoil," and he chided Godey, "You could of had the same if you hadn't got ahead of yourself."

Godey smiled slyly. "I hain't so bad off," he said.

Night caught them on Saluda Mountain in North Carolina. Pockets of fog appeared, and sometimes Riar had to drive with his head through the door. As they crept upward, vehicles passed them, and Godey taunted, "I want to know is this the fastest you can travel?"

"She'd show life," said Mal, "was she fed the gas."

Riar grunted. He was getting used to their gibes.

"Did I have Riar's money," Godey said, "I'd buy me a ten-wheeler. I'd haul a barrel to his peck, put him out of the running."

"They'd no moss grow on the tires either," said Mal.

Riar said, "I'll have to see a profit this trip or I'm already finished. Folks won't have it, but I'm poor as a whippoorwill. I started with nothing, and I'm still in the same fix. You've no reckoning how much a family can run through."

"If I owned a truck," Godey mused, "I'd put in a scat gear, and I'd get gone. I'd whip around curves like a caterpillar. And when I stopped smelling fresh paint I'd trade in on another'n."

Riar said, "The most I can see you possessing is a bigger foot to step on the gas. Your life long you'll be as penniless as you are now."

Nudging Mal, Godey told Riar, "I won't be broke after you and me do a little trafficking."

"You haven't a thing coming from me," said Riar.

"You'll learn different in a minute," said Godey, "for I aim to buy a stack of hamburgers a span high at the next eating place."

"Can't I beat into you we're carrying food?"

Godey said, "I've missed many a bucket of slop, not being a hog." Then he announced, "I'm about to offer you a chance too good to refuse."

"What are you hatching?" asked Riar.

"I'm telling you five bushels of my own peaches are riding in a corner of the rack. They make yours look like drops."

Riar straightened, suddenly vigilant.

Said Mal, "They're Georgia Belles, the ten-cent apiece kind, size of yore fist."

"They sell two dollars a bushel at the shed," boasted Godey, "and they'll peddle for three. I'll let you have the whole caboodle for five bucks."

"Awfulest bargain ever was," said Mal.

"A pure giveaway," said Godey.

Riar's shoe jiggled on the accelerator, the engine coughed. He blurted, "You've got me hauling stolen goods, aye?"

"Dadburn," Godey swore, "I swapped my knife for them and they're mine."

"You didn't trade with the owner," accused Riar. "I'll not reward chicanery."

Godey's lips curled, but he spoke levelly. "I'm a plain talker, and I'm telling you to your teeth I'll not be slicked out of them."

Mal cautioned Riar, "Was I you, I wouldn't cross Godey Spurlock."

"The truth won't hold still," said Riar.

"By jacks," snarled Godey, "you don't know when you're well off."

"Now, no," said Mal.

"I have my principles," said Riar. "What I get for the Belles I'll return to the owner next season."

Godey said, "Anybody with one eye and half sense would understand they couldn't gyp me and prosper."

"You heard me," said Riar.

"You hain't deef," replied Godey.

They hushed. Nothing was said until the lights of Flat Rock appeared. Mal broke the silence, declaring, "I can smell hamburgers clear to here."

Godey mumbled, "I'm so starved I'm growing together."

"Reach back and get some fruit," Riar said irritably. "All you want."

"Juice is oozing out of my ears already," spurned Godey. And he said, "Big Bud, I'm about to make you a final offer. Let me drive to the Tennessee line and you can have my peaches. I'd ruther drive than eat."

"You're not talking to me," said Riar. "I've had a sample of you at the wheel."

"I'll stay on my side of the road, act to suit you."

"Everything has a stopping point," said Riar. "I'll not court a wreck."

"My opinion," said Godey, "when affairs get tough enough you'll break over."

Godey and Mal ate in a café while Riar munched cold bread outside. Before setting off again, Godey held a match to the gasoline meter and said, "You'd better take on a gill. She's sort of low."

"She can read empty," said Riar, "and still be carrying a

gallon." Godey would bear watching.

"See do the tires need wind."

"They're standing up," said Riar, pressing the starter.

Riar didn't pause until he reached Fletcher. He had the tank brimmed, for businesses open after midnight were scarce. And he tightened the cap himself. He climbed the rack, the while cocking an eye at Godey. Riar watched Godey so closely Mal had to do the mischief. Mal caught a chance and scooped up a fistful of dirt, crammed it into the tank, and stuck the cap back on.

They passed through Arden and Skyland and Asheville. And nothing happened. The truck ran smoothly. At Weaverville, Riar halted at a closed station to replenish the radiator. A bulb inside threw a faint light. He left the engine idling, but as he poured in water it quit, and feeling for the key a moment later, he found it missing. He spoke sharply: "All right, you boys, hand over."

"Hand what over?" Godey made strange.

"The key. You don't have to ask."

"Why hallo to us. We haven't got it."

Riar struck a match and searched the cab. He blustered, "I don't want to start war with you fellers."

Stretching, Godey inquired, "Are you of a notion we stole the key? You can frisk us." They stepped out and shucked their pockets.

Mal said, "I never tipped it."

"Couldn't have disappeared of itself," said Riar. "One of you is guilty, and I think I know which."

Godey chuckled sleepily. "Why, it might be square under your nose. Scratch around, keep a-looking."

Riar made a second search, and then he said, "Let me tell you boys something. A load of peaches generates enough heat a day to melt a thousand pounds of ice. They have to be kept moving or they'll bake."

"That makes it mean," said Godey.

"Rough as a cob," agreed Mal.

Riar couldn't budge them. He had no choice other than to

wire-over the ignition. He got out pliers and a screwdriver, but it was pitch-black under the hood. Offering a penny matchbox to Mal, he said, "Strike them for me as they're needed."

"Do that," warned Godey, "and I'll hang you to a bush."

Breathing deep to master his anger, Riar chuffed, "You jaspers don't care whether my family starves."

"Not our lookout," said Godey, yawning.

Lighting match after match, Riar peered to the farthest the key could have been tossed. He felt along the cab floor again and on the ground beneath. When the matchbox was empty he groped with his fingers.

Godey and Mal were soon asleep, but Riar didn't leave off hunting the rest of the night.

At daybreak Riar loosened the ignition wires and hooked them together. The boys stirred as the truck moved, but did not rouse. Beyond the town limits Riar smartened his speed to an unaccustomed forty-five miles an hour. Then, on the grade north of Faust, the engine started missing, and he had to pump the accelerator to coax it to the top.

Halting in the gap, Riar decided gasoline was not getting through to the carburetor, and inspecting the sediment bulb, he found it choked. His breath caught as he reasoned he had been sold dirty gasoline. In a hurry he cleared the bulb and blew out the fuel pump. Already the truck bed seeped juice and the load was drawing hornets. The day had set in hot.

He rolled down hill, and at the bottom it was the same thing over. The engine coughed and lost power. Again the bulb was plugged, the pump fouled. This time he checked the tank, and the deed was out. The cap barely hung on, and the pipe was rimed with grit. Riar gasped. His face reddened in sudden anger. He threw open the cranky door and glared at Godey and Mal. For a moment he had no voice to speak, but when he could he cried, "You boys think you're pistol balls!"

Godey and Mal cracked their eyelids. Godey asked, "What are you looking so dim about?"

Riar sputtered, "You're too sorry to stomp into the ground."

"Has she tuck the studs on you?"

"Filled my tank with dirt. Intending to make me lose my peaches."

"Are you accusing us? Daggone! To hear you tell it, whatever happens to your old scrap heap we're the cause."

"Don't deny it. You're the very scamp."

"If you mean me," said Godey, "that's where you're wrong. Bring me a Scripture and I'll swear by it."

The veins on Riar's neck showed knots. His cheeks looked raw. "Then you put your partner up to it. Besides, you got my key last night."

Godey chirped, "Where's your proof, Tightwad?"

"I have evidence a-plenty," bumbled Riar.

"I'd take oath," vowed Mal, "I never tipped the key."

"When I get mad," confided Godey, "I can see little devils hopping in front of my eyes. How does it serve you?"

Riar was getting nowhere. Slamming the door, he went to work on the pump. He saw the cure was to purge the whole fuel system with fresh gasoline. But getting to a filling station was the question. He tried again and the engine struggled almost a mile before dying.

Godey said, "Give me justice on my peaches and we'll help."

"All you're good for is to gum up," blared Riar. "You're as useless as tits on a boar."

Godey shrugged. He sang, "Suit yourself and sit on the shelf."

"Don't contrary me," Riar begged. "You make me speak things I don't want to."

"Then hurry and fix the old plug, and let's get to some breakfast."

The sun beat upon the peaches as Riar labored. He jock-eyed the truck two miles after unclogging it, a half mile next, and each holdup used three quarters of an hour at least. Then several blowings gained less than five miles altogether, and mid-morning found them still in North Carolina and no station in sight. As the day advanced the load settled slowly, the seep of juice became a trickle. Hornets swarmed, and the fainting fruit seemed to beget gnats. Around eleven the truck made a spurt, crossing into Tennessee jerking and backfiring.

They reached a garage at noon. The mechanic came squinting into the sunlight, inquiring, "What's the matter?"

Godey said, "We've run out of distance."

Riar did the job himself, sweat glistening his face and darkening his shirt. He unstrapped the tank and drained it, flushed it with water, and rinsed in gasoline. He removed the fuel line, pump, and carburetor and gave them the same treatment. The mechanic said, "If I had a pump messed up like that I'd junk it and buy a new."

Godey laughed. "Did this gentleman turn loose a dollar the hide would slip."

While Riar strove, he knew without looking that the lower half of the load was crushing under the weight, the top layers sickening in the sun. The hundred or so bushels in between would hold firm only a few hours longer, and he would never get them to Kentucky. He would have to try selling them in the next town.

Toward three o'clock Riar finished and set off grimly, raising his speed to fifty miles an hour. The machine would go no faster.

Godey crowed, "The old sister will travel if you'll feed her. Pour on the pedal."

Mal asked wryly, "Reckon she'll take another Jiminy fit?"

"Stay on the whiz," cheered Godey, "and maybe she'll shed the rust."

It was fortunate that a rise had slowed them when the tire blew out. As it was, Riar had to fight the wheel to keep to the road. He brought the truck under control and pulled onto a shoulder. He sat as if stricken, his disgust too great for speaking. His stomach began to cramp. Presently he said bitterly, "I hope this satisfies your hickory."

Godey and Mal wagged their heads, though their faces were bright. Godey said, "I reckon it's us you'll blame."

Mal said, "Everything that pops he figures we're guilty."

"Your talk and your actions don't jibe," Riar suffered himself to speak.

On examining the flat, Riar discovered a slash in the tread as straight as a blade could make it. He walked numbly around the truck and took a look at the Elbertas. They had fallen seven slats, the firm peaches sinking into the pulp of the bad, and they were working alive with gnats and hornets. They would bluff any buyer. He said, "You have destroyed me."

"What do you think I'm getting from the trip?" asked Godey. "Nothing but a hole in my breeches."

Riar said, "I'm ruint, ruint totally."

"Tightwads never fill their barrels," blabbed Godey. "They want more."

Riar swallowed. His stomach seemed balled. "I swear to my Maker," he said, "you have the heart of a lizard." He took his time repairing the tube, using a cold patch and covering it with a boot. He idled, trying to feel better. The shade was over when they started again.

Godey asked, "What are you going to do now?"

Riar was long replying. Finally he said, "If I've burned a blister I'm willing to set on it."

They entered Virginia at dusk, and the evening was hardly less torrid than the day. Ground mist cloaked the road like steam. The boys were snoring by the time they reached Wise.

The enormity of his loss came upon Riar as he neared Kentucky. Cramps nearly doubled him. When he could endure no more he pulled off and cut the lights, and leaving the truck, he walked up the highway in the dark. He pursed his lips and whistled tunelessly. He strolled several hundred yards before turning back.

Riar dumped the peaches at the foot of Pound Mountain. Once he thought he heard his key jingle but was mistaken, for he discovered it later inside the cushion.

It occurred to him that a little food might quiet his stomach, but rummaging the toolbox he found the last crumb gone. He came upon the fuzz and lifted the poke to get rid of it but still didn't let loose. Stepping into the cab he switched on the lights. Godey and Mal slept with heads pitched forward, collars agape. Their faces were yellow as cheese pumpkins in the reflected gleam. Riar untied the poke and shook the fuzz down their necks.

For a distance up the mountain the trees were woolly with fog, but as the truck climbed the mist vanished and the heat fell away. Riar's spirits rose as he mounted, the cramping ceased. The engine pulled the livelier. They had crossed the Kentucky line in the gap and were headed down when the boys began to wriggle.

# Afterword

After six years of schoolkeeping at the forks of Troublesome Creek in Knott County, I moved nine miles farther back in the hills to a century-old log house between the waters of Dead Mare Branch and Wolfpen, on Little Carr Creek. These streams boxed me in. I raised my own food and stored vegetables and fruits for the cold months; I kept two stands of bees for their honey, and for the ancient custom of "telling the bees."

In those days the post office was called Bath, named after the oldest Roman town in England, and the mail carrier travelled on horseback. I joined the folk life of the scattered community, attending church meetings, funeralizings, corn pullings, hog butcherings, box suppers at the one-room school, sapping parties, and gingerbread elections. There were two goods stores within walking distance, one at the foot of Little Carr, the other a mile above. These were the social centers where local happenings and human doings were discussed.

A neighbor said of me, "He's quit a good job and come over in here and just sot down." I did sit down and finished writing the novel *River of Earth*. And I wrote many a poem and short story, most of which found their way into national publications. A number of the stories were reprinted in *Best American Short Stories* and in *O. Henry Memorial Prize Stories*. One gained an award.

My writings drew on everyday experiences and observations. I only wrote when an idea overwhelmed me. Such as when the waters of Dead Mare Branch dried in August to a

series of diminishing potholes of water, crowded with minnows. Although I drew water from my well and replenished
the holes daily, it was to little avail. Few survived until a rain
could wash them to the freedom of Little Carr.

### LEAP MINNOWS, LEAP

*The minnows leap in drying pools.*
*In islands of water along the creekbed sands*
*They spring on drying tails, white bellies to the sun,*
*Gills spread, gills fevered and gasping.*
*The creek is sun and sand, and fish throats rasping.*

*One pool has a peck of minnows. One living pool*
*Is knuckle deep with dying, a shrinking yard*
*Of glittering bellies. A thousand eyes look, look,*
*A thousand gills strain, strain the water-air.*

*There is plenty of water above the dam, locked and deep,*
*Plenty, plenty and held. It is not here.*
*It is not where the minnows spring with lidless fear.*
*They die as men die. Leap minnows, leap.*

Besides growing my own food, I introduced vegetables
new to the area. And I began experiments with the wild
strawberry and the wild violet, an attempt by natural selec-
tion to discover superior plants. The leaf-miner became a
subject of study. I found John Muir's observations sound:
"When we try to pick out anything by itself, we find it
hitched to everything else in the universe." My lamp-lit eve-
nings were spent reading in the fields of literature, history,
and science. The classical age in Greece, the American Civil
War, and primitive life the world over interested me. The
library of Virginia Polytechnic Institute supplied by mail any
book I wished to borrow.

Although my stories and poems were appearing in *The
Atlantic, The Yale Review, The Virginia Quarterly Review,*
and a variety of other publications and I had three published

books, I do not recall encountering anybody during those years who had read them. I wrote in an isolation which was virtually total. Whether that was good or bad I cannot say. More than one rescue party came to try to persuade me back to "civilization." I didn't leave for any period of time until I joined the army in 1941. I was on another continent and longing for home when I pencilled this verse of recollection:

*How it was in that place, how light hung in a bright pool*
*Of air like water, in an eddy of cloud and sky,*
*I will long remember. I will long recall*
*The maples blossoming birds, the oaks proud with rule,*
*The spiders deep in silk, the squirrels fat on mast,*
*The fields and draws and coves where quail and peewees call.*
*Earth loved more than any earth, stand firm, hold fast;*
*Trees burdened with leaf and wing, root deep, grow tall.*

When I moved from Troublesome Creek to the backwoods of the county I had expected to stay only for a summer. I have remained forty years. As the past withdraws it may be that the stories in this volume amount to a social diagram of a folk society such as hardly exists today and may even include some of the uncharted aspects of the Appalachian experience.

JAMES STILL